CHOICES

To
Hope you enjoy
this!
All the Best
Celia

C.H. HEALY

C. H. Healy.

Dedicated
To The Memory of
Barry Fisher

My Earthbound Angel

INTRODUCTION

People will often refer to their future using words like fate, destiny, superstition, intuition, timing, kismet, etc., but deep down inside they don't like the thought of their path already being chosen for them. They prefer to believe that they are the authors of their own future. So when they have a choice to make, no matter how minor it may seem, how can they possibly predict the influence *that* choice may have on future events in their lives or the lives of others? What do you call it when you have no control over the events that affect your life? If certain events occur that you had no choice in, does that mean that someone or something else is deciding what course your path will take? In some circles it's even believed that a person chooses the parents they want to be born to. If that's true, then how is it that we can't predict our own future; or can we? There are the everyday choices such as the ones between good and bad, right and wrong, left and right, up and down. But when faced with a decision of enormous magnitude people will often ask "the powers that *be*" for a sign. Some sort of guidance in making the right choice or decision, but then doesn't this mean they are still leaving their fate in someone else's hands?

CHAPTER 1

While driving home from an interview with a new client, Jordan found herself completely taken in by the sunshine and fresh air of the mid-summer day while she made her way through traffic on the busy boulevard. As she approached the outskirts of her neighborhood, she suddenly heard a song on the radio that was totally befitting to the ambiance of the day and she turned the volume up so she could sing along. While tapping her fingers on the steering wheel in tune with the music she pulled up to a stop sign. Just as she was about to reaccelerate a young man in a business suit and riding a bicycle came bounding out of nowhere. She immediately slammed on the brakes, but not in time to avoid nudging him and knocking him off of his bike. She quickly put the car in park and got out to see if he was okay. As she approached him he hurriedly got up, looked at his watch, dusted off his knees and mounted his bike. As he and his bike wobbled away from her, he assured her several times that he was alright but couldn't stop or he would be late.

She watched him for a few seconds until he disappeared from sight while still waving her off and repeating that he was fine. Realizing that there was nothing she could do to change the situation, she slightly lowered her head and grinned to herself as she bit her lower lip and envisioned Alice in Wonderland when she came across the white rabbit. Suddenly the fairy tale was over as Jordan was startled by the honking of a horn. When she spun around she saw that she was holding up another vehicle at the stop sign so she motioned him to go around her as she quickly returned to her car to try to make sense of what just occurred. While she sat there trying to replay in her mind what just happened, her hands suddenly started to shake and then her whole body started to tremble with the realization of what *almost* happened.

There was a little neighborhood bistro / bar around the corner that Jordan would sometimes meet new clients at and she decided that now would be a good time to stop by and have a drink to try to settle her nerves. The staff there knew her well but they were surprised to see her so early in the day. Making light of the situation with dramatizations and hand gestures, she jokingly related to them what had just happened and said she was going to use it as an excuse to have a drink before five o'clock. They laughingly took her order and the owner even threw in a plate of appetizers on the house. Because it was such a beautiful day, she chose to sit on the patio thinking that the fresh air would help to clear her head and stop the butterflies inside her from reproducing.

She observed how strange everything seemed to be in the middle of the day compared to the late afternoon or early evening when she usually frequents this little establishment. Taking a few minutes to relax as she took the first taste of her mid-day cocktail, she looked out over her surroundings and couldn't help but notice all the different little nuances. There were flowers in bloom that she never noticed before and their fragrances filled the air. There were also a variety of people passing by and even seated in the bistro that were of a different sort than the usual dinner and evening crowds that she was used to seeing.   Suddenly she noticed a little boy walking along with whom she could only assume was his little sister in tow. He held her hand like a vise as they approached the corner and spent several minutes looking up and down the street before crossing it. As she watched the care and attention this little boy displayed for his sister, she couldn't help but think back to her own beginnings.

Jordan was not unlike a lot of other single women her age. Average height and looks, good moral fabric, strong work ethics, and an overwhelming dislike for being told what to do. All that made it easy for her to choose the path her career had taken in being her own boss. She had tried her hand at a variety of jobs but when she worked at the land titles office for three years she discovered that she had a knack for being able to uncover what had been hidden, sometimes on purpose. Now she made a decent living as a research consultant and companies actually paid her to unlock the secrets of the universe. Well . . . maybe not to that extent but nonetheless, she was doing what she truly loved and was good at.

She never really understood where her love of the unknown came from because she didn't remember a lot about her parents *or* her childhood. All she could really remember of her mother was the gentle touch of her hands. She had a loving and reassuring touch that Jordan had carried with her all these years. Her father died two weeks before her sixth birthday and she lost her mother shortly after that. Her earliest memories were of her dad but she could only remember him through the eyes of a six-year-old little girl. Sometimes she had trouble picturing what he looked like but she *did* remember staring into his eyes and knowing that he would always take care of her. He was a hard working man but his rough and callused hands somehow had the gentlest touch and always made her feel loved and safe.

Her father worked for the county highway department as a grader operator and came home every day just wanting to be with his family. Jordan could always tell when he was expected home by the mouthwatering aromas that came wafting from the kitchen as her mom prepared her dad's favorite foods for dinner. That was Jordan's cue to run to the front door and watch for his truck to pull into the driveway. When she thought back to that time she could see herself peering through the bottom of the screen door and remembered how big everything looked. She also remembered how she could only hear the sound of her own breathing as she anxiously waited for her daddy, then the feeling of absolute glee as he finally pulled up to the house.

She was too young to know it then but all he really wanted to do was to have a shower and relax. Instead, he would swoop her up in his arms and they would sit together on the front step and watch everything and everybody that passed by: planes, cars, birds, clouds, bikes, people - it didn't matter, they all had a story. He would always ask her where *she* thought they were going and how *she* thought they got there. As he listened, he would have a subtle little smile on his lips and marvel at the sight of that wide-eyed little girl as she babbled on about the magic that she imaged was involved.

One day the phone rang and her mommy dropped to her knees and cried. Her daddy never came home that day . . . or ever again. Jordan had a brother named Dalton who was four years older than her and from that day on, he became her protector. Their mom never stopped crying and eventually people, a lot of people, came to the house and then her mommy went away too. Jordan never understood what happened and the trauma of those events and what transpired over the next few years had been buried in the deepest recesses of her soul.

Jordan and Dalton found themselves being placed in different foster homes over the next several months but they were always together. Dalton often had to hold her at night when her nightmares would wake her up and he would tenderly rub her back as she drifted back to sleep. Today, she can't remember what the dreams were about but she did remember staring up at Dalton and feeling as safe as she did when she looked into her daddy's eyes. Dalton had one hazel colored eye and one blue colored eye. He used to tell her that one was for daytime and one was for nighttime, that way he could always watch over her no matter what time of day it was. *That* explanation was good enough for a little girl her age and made her feel protected and not so alone.

Eventually, Jordan and Dalton were separated and they sent her off to a different foster home. She had no way of knowing it then but apparently it was difficult to keep siblings together within the system, especially ones of different genders and such an age difference. Jordan soon realized that she was all alone and it wasn't long before she withdrew within herself with just her nightmares to keep her company.

When Jordan was eight years old, a woman appeared at her foster home claiming to be her daddy's sister. Jordan's mother was an only child and her father was also one of two children. Her dad's parents had a great sense of ancestry and heritage so they went back generations when naming their children. Her dad was christened Thane and his sister Tallulah. Jordan went home with her Aunt Tilley that day, but the nightmares continued over the next few years.

Aunt Tilley could best be described as a modern day "Auntie Mame", only with a little more of a spiritual flare. Tilley never married and spent most of her life traveling the world. She had been on a spiritual retreat in the Himalayas when she heard of her brother's passing. Unfortunately, quite some time had already elapsed, but as soon as she got word she made her way back home. After a couple more years of fighting the courts, bureaucrats, and red tape, she was finally able to track down Jordan, however the system had lost track of Dalton after he ran away from his foster home when he was twelve. Tilley had continued her search for him and had exhausted nearly all her resources trying to find him until she had no choice but to give up her quest and concentrate on Jordan.

She raised Jordan and educated her in ways that none of the educational facilities that she attended could have. She possessed a quick wit with an incredible sense of humor and Jordan always thought of her as her very own "Confucius". She always had *some* pearls of wisdom for every situation that arose, which taught Jordan to think outside the box and allowed her to see the other side of most things. Tilley's philosophy was the grass is *not* always greener on the other side . . . most times they just use more fertilizer. Jordon always smiled when she remembered that quote because she was a full-grown adult before she really understood its meaning. When it came right down to it though, Jordan was always encouraged to make her own decisions.

While sitting on the patio of the bistro that day and watching the little boy holding his sister's hand, Jordan decided that maybe it was time to put some of her own God-given talents to good use and pick up where Tilley had left off years ago. It was time for Jordan to try to find her brother. After all, they say that everybody knows everybody by six degrees of separation. All she had to do was find those other six people.

CHAPTER 2

Jordan had left the bistro and made her way home, but upon arriving there she realized that she was almost in a daze as she unlocked her door. She barely remembered the drive home and was still in a state of confusion as she kicked off her shoes and slouched onto her couch. Once Jordan had decided to look for Dalton she became very excited with the prospect of seeing her big brother again but her mind was being flooded with questions that had no answers: where do I start . . . what if he doesn't want to be found . . . what kind of man would he be today . . . what kind of home did he grow up in . . . would he remember me . . . had he been looking for me at all over the years?

Jordan heaved a big sigh and without thinking, reached out to the coffee table and picked up a picture of her and Tilley. It was taken by a neighbor at the surprise barbeque Tilley threw for Jordan's sixteenth birthday. Jordan found herself getting completely lost in the picture and vividly recalled every moment of that day. Just two days before, she had locked herself in her bedroom and swore she was never coming out because her boyfriend of two weeks had just dumped her. She was devastated! Tilley tried everything she could to reassure her that "life will go on". Jordan remembers being so angry with her aunt when she said, "Oh my little one . . . if this is the worst thing that ever happens to you – I will be *so* happy." That statement seemed so cruel at the time but now seemed so wise. It took her years to realize that her aunt was right . . . things could always be worse.

Tilley had invited all of Jordan's friends and everyone within a three block radius to the surprise outdoor birthday party she had planned to celebrate her niece's special birthday. She even set up a couple of tables with ritual statues and carvings from different native tribes she had encountered on her many excursions that demonstrated a young girl's rite of passage into womanhood. These tables were also the setting of traditional dishes that were supposed to help nourish the soul along its journey. All of Jordan's friends thought Tilley was the "coolest" and never tired with her stories of worldly adventures. Jordan still hadn't been in a party frame of mind that day but grudgingly made an appearance thinking how unfair it was that not everyone was sensitive to her pain . . . typical sixteen year old. Then it happened . . . as the crowd parted and the sun came out, she saw him standing there; leather vest, tee shirt with the sleeves ripped out, sparkling smile, ripped jeans, greasy curly hair, cigarette behind one ear, and as their eyes met and her heart started to sing with joy . . . (oh crap – what was his name again?) Jordan shook her head to bring herself back to the here and now and smiled as she tried to remember the name of the neighbor's nephew that came to her party that day. It was mostly because of him that she remembered that day so fondly, plus the fact that she never gave what's-his-name from two days previous another thought.

Reminiscing wasn't going to help find her brother so Jordan decided to give Tilley a call, hoping that perhaps her aunt could shed some light on this dilemma. Most of all . . . she just felt the need to receive Tilley's blessing before she could move forward.

Sitting alone in her condo, Jordan tried to find the last number she had for her aunt, not really knowing what she would do next if the number was no longer in service. Sending her an e-mail might take days to get a response. Tilley had returned to her globe-trotting life after Jordan graduated from college and moved away from home. They kept in touch over the years mostly through technology, but Tilley always called Jordan on her birthday, which would be followed by a parcel sent from somewhere in the world. She never worried about keeping track of a phone number for her aunt because she moved around so much, so she was positively delighted to hear Tilley's voice message when she finally found the last number she had for her aunt.

Jordan left a message reassuring Tilley that she was alright and everything was fine, but she needed to talk to her about a personal issue that was important. She briefly conveyed her intentions and wanted to know how she felt about her plan, then asked her to get back to her as soon as she could.

Jordan had to start somewhere so she put a call into a friend who worked at the Department of Motor Vehicles and asked if he could do a search for her brother. Then she spent the rest of the evening on the internet searching the usual sites for "finding people". She couldn't help thinking how wonderful it would be if her friend could find Dalton through his driver's license or even if he was registered on one of these sites and would be easy to find. Jordan wasn't lazy but when she wanted something – she wanted it *now*! After several hours her search of the "world wide web" was in vain, so she held on to the hope that her friend at the DMV would have more luck. She was, however, able to gather a lot of information on the process of locating someone who might be registered within the system, and compiled a list of agencies with contact names and numbers. She also discovered that this process of coarse would only apply to those who wanted to be found. She left e-mail messages on the sites that encouraged that sort of thing with hopes that someone would respond shortly with any information that might help.

It was getting late but Jordan couldn't bring herself to take a break. With so much information available on the net, she almost became obsessed with absorbing as much as she could. All of a sudden she heard a thunderous pounding that made her sit up straight and with her heart in her throat she could feel and hear her own chest pounding just as loud as the noise that seemed to be all around her. She had fallen asleep at the computer and someone was impatiently hammering at her door. After feeling a little disoriented she collected her composure, shook off the initial shock, and tried to clear the thickness in her head while she hurried to the door ready to blast whoever it was for causing such a ruckus.

She was horrified to see Tilley standing there holding a bag of bagels and two large coffees.

"It's about time you opened the door little one, I've been knocking for five minutes." Tilley quickly made her way past Jordan with a kiss on her cheek as she flew into the room in grand "Tilley" style. She placed a cup of cappuccino in Jordan's hand as she made her way to the dining room table.

Jordan stood there in disbelief staring at the cup of coffee and thinking that she must still be asleep and this was all a dream.

"But how . . ." was all Jordan was able to utter before Tilley chimed in.

"Oh that nice young man that lives down the hall from you let me in downstairs. Did you know that he works the graveyard shift for one week out of every month and usually sees you leaving for work as he's coming home? That's how I ran into him – he was just getting off shift. I got the impression that he looks forward to seeing you during that week. Have you ever thought of asking him out?"

Jordan was still standing there with her mouth hanging open and not believing her eyes. She blinked a few times, shook her head and said "*No*! . . . I mean . . . I don't know . . . I mean . . . who are you talking about? Tilley – what are you doing here? How did you get here so fast?"

As Tilley unwrapped the bagels, placed a large valise on the table, and hung her sweater on the back of one of the chairs – she explained. "You're not going to believe this but two days ago I was offered the chance to go to Indonesia to visit with a 109-year-old shaman who still rides his bike up the mountain pass every day to get to the spot where he meditates. I *just* had a feeling that I should stop by the house and get my smudging feathers, 'cause you know how they always bring me luck, and that's where I was headed when I got your message. So instead, when I got home, I packed up all the paperwork I had kept from when I had tried to find your brother just in case there might be something there that you can use, then took the commuter flight here this morning . . . did you sleep in those clothes? I thought I raised you better than that. Where are your plates? I have some spinach cream cheese for the bagels that is to die for . . . and don't worry about the shaman sweetie – he's been there for over a century and I'm sure he'll be there a while longer - so tell me little one . . . what happened to make you pick up the gauntlet now for this journey of yours - because you never wanted to talk about it before".

Jordan thought about it for a minute and realized that, as usual, Tilley was right. Every time the subject of Dalton came up in the past Jordan would just "shut down" and refuse to discuss it. She sat down with Tilley and related the events of the other day. Jordan had never been one for wearing her heart on her sleeve so it was a little difficult describing the emotions she experienced during the few minutes she sat and watched the two children waiting to cross the street. As Jordan stumbled for the right words, Tilley sat motionless and listened with great interest as her niece related how she felt as she watched that little boy and his sister.

"Now that I think of it . . . it was always too painful to remember Dalton but seeing those two children made me remember the love instead of the pain."

"Well . . . I guess it was a sign that now you're ready for *this* chapter in your life."

"Oh Tilley . . . you don't still believe that fate or destiny has a hand in everything that happens do you?"

"Absolutely! Everything happens for a reason girl . . . you know that! For example, why else would I have been on my way home for the first time in over a year just to pick up some feathers that have been in storage for a decade. They *do* have birds in Indonesia ya' know – I'm sure I even could've gotten some eagle feathers there. It was a sign . . . a sign that I'm supposed to be right here, right now, with you."

Jordan stared at her aunt while she took a deep breath and not wanting to get into this discussion right now, just wrapped her arms around her. The two of them embraced for a few minutes until Tilley insisted they get a hold of themselves before the tears started. The two of them went out to the terrace with their coffees and bagels with cream cheese, and then spent the rest of the day catching up and trying to strategize a plan of action. Tilley pulled out hoards of papers to show Jordan what she had tried in the past hoping it would give them some insight as to where to start their search. While looking over some of the documents, Jordan realized that Tilley already had most of the information that she had found on the internet the night before. Then an icy chill ran over her as she realized that some of them were dated within the past couple of years and she looked up at Tilley with tears in her eyes.

"Why didn't you tell me you never gave up looking for him?"

Tilley sat up straight, took Jordan's hands in hers and looked her right in the eyes as she tried to explain.

"At first it was because I knew it was too painful for you and *then* it was because I didn't want to get your hopes up. As more time went by and finding an adult with no history of a past . . . well - it started to seem hopeless so I didn't want to burden you with it. I knew there would come a time when you would be ready. I just prayed that I would be around for this day . . . now where do you want to start?"

CHAPTER 3

The two women spent the next day comparing notes. Between the files that Tilley had kept and what Jordan had learned from the internet they felt pretty good about what direction they should start in. That evening they decided to visit Jordan's little bistro where it had all began and drink a toast to their new beginning. The weather was still mild so Jordan was delighted that they were able to sit out on the patio again so she could walk Tilley through the events of that day that she was hoping would change her life. Jordan was excited as she described to Tilley what she had felt while watching the little boy and his sister. As they relaxed and talked about the past, Jordan realized that her mind was finally at ease and she felt confident about the journey they were getting ready to embark on. Tilley always had a calming effect on Jordan, so she was very grateful that her aunt had decided to be there with her.

All of a sudden Tilley sat back and with one eyebrow raised and her head cocked to one side she sat motionless as she stared at her niece. Jordan was *shocked* – she remembered that look but hadn't seen it for years - she usually got it when she had done something wrong.

"What?" Jordan exclaimed.

"You didn't even notice . . . did you?" Tilley asked as she folded her arms across her chest.

"Notice what?"

"That nice young man waiting on us has been hovering over you since we sat down and you've barely acknowledged him."

Jordan looked around and spotted the man Tilley was talking about and said, "Gene? . . . what do you mean? I thanked him when he filled my water glass."

"Yes – you've been polite, but that's not what I'm talking about. Haven't you noticed the way he looks at you? Do you even know anything about him?"

"Of course I do . . . he's one of the owners and I see him every time I come in here – he's a nice guy and always makes me feel welcome, but that's his job".

"Oh really . . . how many "*owners*" do you know that would wait around to be at *your* beck and call . . . do you see him filling any one else's water glass?"

Jordan slowly surveyed the bistro and realized that again, Tilley was right. Gene was standing at the end of the bar going over receipts while his staff was busy seeing to the needs of all the other customers. All of a sudden he looked up and caught her staring at him and within the blink of an eye he was at their table asking if they needed anything. This made Jordan very uncomfortable and she found herself acting like a schoolgirl, not knowing what to say next. She made up something and fumbled for the words to ask a question about the menu, which she was certain he saw right through because she knew the menu like the back of her hand. He smiled and answered her question then looked at Tilley with a little grin and she quickly offered her hand and introduced herself. Gene leaned over and accepted Tilley's gesture by not only shaking her hand but holding it with both of his as he told her what a pleasure it was to meet her. He related the fact that

15

Jordan had never spoken about her family. He also expressed concern that he thought she worked too hard and that it was such a joy to see her there with someone other than a client.

Jordan couldn't help but wonder how he knew so much about her . . . and why she had never noticed that he had such an amazing smile. She suddenly realized that she had never really looked at him before. He was just always *there*.

Tilley was completely taken aback by Gene and the two of them bantered back and forth about Jordan's personal and professional life. Jordan wasn't really paying attention to what they were talking about because all she could hear was the rush of blood through her ears. She was feeling more and more like she did when she was in high school every time a boy would come calling and Tilley would work her magic to find out everything about him before giving her blessing. She always ended up allowing the date so Jordan never understood why the third degree was necessary. Thinking back on it. . . Jordan realized that Tilley never objected to any of the boys that came around. No matter how much of a "rebel" they seemed to be, Tilley would never deny Jordan the right to go out with whomever she wanted. It was like her aunt always knew that they were just a phase that her niece was going through and she would always be there to pick up the pieces when the infatuation ended. Jordan always respected her aunt for that and the fact that not once did she ever say "I told you so".

When Gene finally left their table Tilley burst into laughter. As she dabbed the corners of her eyes with her napkin and caught her breath she said, "I can't believe what I just saw – you were actually at a loss for words! You should see the look on your face! It's priceless!"

Now Jordan was really embarrassed and turned her head to take a sip of water hoping that no one else could see the many shades of red that were washing over her cheeks.

The two of them giggled for a couple more minutes and Jordan remembered how good it was to laugh out loud again. She hadn't realized how much she missed Tilley and the lighthearted way she looked at life. It was so good to be with her again even if Tilley *was* enjoying Jordan's embarrassment just a little too much.

Having Tilley around made Jordan aware of just how badly she had been wrapped up in her own life, especially in her work. It was to the point where she had almost forgotten how to live. As if someone had opened a door and let the light in, she almost felt exposed as she realized that she hadn't thought of anything or anyone else but her own existence for years. Now her head was up and she was seeing at lot of things for the first time. For instance, she never noticed how nice Gene was before, why couldn't she and Tilley talk more than a couple of times a year, and . . . who *is* this guy that lived down the hall from her? With all this new activity running through her head, Jordan realized that it's not all about her and all of a sudden her thoughts were wrapped around Tilley. She had never really thought about it before but . . . she couldn't remember anyone calling on Tilley the whole time she was growing up. This got her thinking . . . why hadn't her aunt ever married?

While they enjoyed their dessert, Jordan asked Tilley if she had ever been in love. There were never any men in her life while she was raising Jordan and she couldn't recall her aunt ever mentioning anyone in a past tense either.

Her aunt was never one for offering information about her personal feelings but she would also never put Jordan off when she asked a question. "Yes – I *have* been in love. I was even engaged at one time. As a matter of fact, that's how I made most of my money."

Jordan was completely dumbfounded and now her curiosity was running wild as she wanted to know more.

"I met him in college. I was completely smitten and fell head-over-heels. He had a Fu Manchu, long curly hair, played the guitar, and defied the system by wearing an earring – my kinda guy. We lived together off campus and every night he would sing to me and we would discuss our plans for changing the world together. He even wrote a song for me and planned to record it someday. He was a business major and was brilliant when it came to the stock market. I was supposed to go home for Thanksgiving one year and he always said that holidays like that were too much like giving into the institution of "The Man" so he didn't want to come with me. Halfway home I decided that I would rather be with him than my family so I turned around and headed back. When I couldn't find him in our flat I went looking for him on campus, thinking that he might be working on a paper or an assignment of some kind. Instead, I found him under a tree in front of the library, strumming his guitar and serenading Molly with *my* song - he just substituted my name for hers. I have to admit that I went through every emotion and stopped when I got to "vengeance". It didn't leave a very pleasant taste in my mouth but I knew there would be an opportunity for me to get back at him for his deceitfulness. Timing is everything and I just had to wait for my turn. I went back to my folk's place for the holiday and a couple of weeks later - I got my chance for revenge. He said he wanted to invest all our savings on a stock he knew about that would set us up for life. At that time, *our* savings was *my* savings . . . after all, they say love is blind and I blindly used that old adage to justify supporting him so he could "focus" on his greatness.

Between what I had saved before I went to college and what I made waiting tables at a local coffee shop and selling hand-made macramé hangers, I had managed to support the two of us and build a little nest egg.   I agreed to give him the money but because I handled all the finances, he never realized that I only gave him a fraction of what I had. He invested it and then cashed the stocks in a month later and took off with Molly. I never saw him again but I heard that after he and Molly got married, she cleaned him out in the divorce – *sweet justice*. That was the first time I really started to believe in karma, what goes around comes around. As much as I no longer trusted him, I did however believe in his insight to the stock market. So unbeknownst to him, I had invested the majority of my remaining savings in the same stock and by the time I sold some of them, I made enough money to put into other investments that contributed to the lifestyle that I now enjoy."

Jordan was completely astounded by the story she just heard and couldn't believe that Tilley had never told it before. "What did you do next?"

"I finished college, got my degree in art history, sold some stocks, and took off to Fiji – where I stayed in hostels and hitchhiked around the country. That was the first time I ever went abroad and I haven't looked back since."

Jordan's head was spinning with this amazing story and after trying to absorb it all she asked, "Was that the only time you were in love?"

"Oh goodness no . . . falling in love is easy. The trick is to take someone with you when you fall and *that's* the part I haven't figured out yet."

"Is it because you're waiting for your "soul mate"?" Jordan asked with a sarcastic little grin as she sipped on her drink.

"*I* don't wait for anybody – if I did, I would never *get* anywhere. But I don't think it's unreasonable to want someone who would need me because he loves me instead of someone who loves me because he needs me . . . so what are *you* waiting for?" Tilley asked with the same sarcasm.

"Have another drink." Jordan said in order to avoid the subject and at the same time try to make sense of the riddle Tilley just threw at her.

Before they knew it, hours had passed and the bistro was closing. This time when Gene came to their table he reiterated how nice it was to see Jordan again and what a pleasure it was meeting Tilley. As he handed them their bill he pointed out that their drinks were on the house and he looked forward to them returning. Jordan looked up at him and smiled while Tilley assured him that they would be back soon. He seemed very pleased to hear that, smiled at them both, then slowly walked back to the bar. Jordan didn't realize that she was watching him walk away until Tilley cleared her throat with a sassy little grin that broke her concentration as they got up to leave.

CHAPTER 4

After a good night's sleep the two women took their morning coffee to the terrace and planned their day. They had come to the conclusion that if they were going to find Dalton, they had to start where they lost him in the first place. Trying to think back to what it was like all those years ago they tried to answer the question "Where would an underaged; and presumably frightened, boy go to during that time frame?"

Tilley had said that back in her day, a boy would run away to the "YMCA". There he would learn how to box and sweep floors for change and a place to sleep. Well, times had changed a little but Jordan thought that she might not be too far off in her theory and figured it might be easier to imagine the state of mind that he would have been in at the time. He had been separated from his sister, whom he vowed to protect, and had no way of knowing where she had been taken to. She was hoping that his mission at the time would be to find his little sister and thinking this way might give them a direction to start in. If it was her and the situation was reversed, she might return home to see if he came back looking for her there.

They loaded up Jordan's car and took a road trip back to their old hometown. It was quite an experience for

Tilley also; after all, this was where she grew up. Her brother Thane never left their quiet little hometown because he married his high school sweetheart and started a family. This also gave Tilley's parents the chance to be closer to their only grandchildren, Jordan and Dalton.

While on the road Jordan's cell phone rang - it was her friend from the DMV. She got very excited when she heard his voice but soon felt deflated when she heard the news he had for her. When his search locally turned up nothing, he expanded it nation-wide but was unable find any record of the name she gave him. He felt really bad about not being able to help her and said that he would be happy to run it again if she came up with any new information. Jordan thanked him profusely and promised to keep in touch, then hung up the phone and told Tilley the news. Now all their hopes rested on finding something when they reached their destination.

As they entered the limits of the old hometown, Tilley was excited and even became a little nostalgic. She commented on several landmarks that had changed or were no longer there, but Jordan was so young when she left that she couldn't remember any of them. The only thing Jordan really remembered were the trips to and from her grandparents and playing in her backyard. All of a sudden Tilley spotted the old water tower by the tracks that ran through where the stockyards used to be and she squealed with delight.

"Ohhh – I can't believe the old water tower is still there! I remember one time when Justin Greene and I climbed up there one night after a football game in junior high and . . . ." She suddenly stopped in mid sentence, turned to look at Jordan, then pursed her lips as if to swallow her words and thought about it for a minute. "Maybe that's a story for another time."

Jordan laughed and at the same time scolded her aunt, "You do that *every* time!"

"What do you mean – every time *what*?"

"Ever since I was a little girl, you would start to tell a story and then stop because you thought it wouldn't be appropriate and then you would say – *I'll tell you some day when you're older.* Just how old do I have to be before you let me in on your past adventures – or will I have to wait and read it in your memoirs?" As Jordan shook a finger at her aunt like a parent would to a misbehaving child she said, "I promise you that when this is all over I want to hear all about them – including the one about the water tower!" and they continued on their way to the old neighborhood.

As they pulled into the driveway of the house that Jordan remembered, an overwhelming urge to break into tears rushed over her. It seemed like the only thing that had changed was the color of the house and the surrounding foliage that had grown. They sat in the car for a couple of minutes so Jordan could collect herself before gathering up the nerve to knock on the front door. As they approached the steps, Jordan couldn't help but notice that things didn't seem quite as big as they did when she was little, then she caught a glimpse of something from the corner of her eye. There, behind the now huge lilac bushes, was the swing that her daddy had made for her. It had a wide wooden seat and super magical ropes to hold her up so she could always come back to earth when she tried to reach the sky while she was swinging. At least, that was the story her daddy told her while he was building it for her.

She took a deep breath and rang the bell. A few seconds later they were greeted by an elderly man with a cane in one hand and a kitchen towel in the other. He graciously smiled and asked if he could help them. Jordan stumbled for the right words, she hadn't really prepared herself for what she would say if someone actually answered the door, nor was she prepared for the emotions that were flooding over her like a tidal wave. Tilley recognized Jordan's anguish right away and took over. She quickly explained who they were and that they were hoping to get some information on the little boy who used to live there. Then she pulled out an old picture of her brother and his family and asked the gentleman if he could think back and remember ever seeing anyone in the photo. Jordan was dumbfounded to see the picture and without wanting to appear ignorant she didn't say a word but quietly looked at Tilley with disbelieving eyes.

Tilley quickly turned to Jordan and softly said, "It was the last picture I got from your mom and dad." Tilley went on to explain to him that the photo was taken around Christmas time shortly before her brother passed away so if he had seen the little boy he would have been about five or six years older than he appeared in the photo. The only thing that would have stood out about him was the fact that he had different colored eyes.

The old gentleman held the photo at arms length and squinted at it for a few seconds then shocked Jordan by suggesting something that you would never consider doing if you live in the city – he introduced himself as Ira and invited the two strange women into his home so he could get his glasses to take a better look at the picture. As they entered, Jordan was overwhelmed with the awe she felt with being home again but the biggest surprise of all was the tantalizing aroma that filled the house. Suddenly she could see into the kitchen where there was a little grey haired lady standing over a table filled with apples. Ira smiled, motioned them in and giving her a peck on the cheek he introduced his wife, Grace. Grace giggled at his boldness and used her apron to dust the flour from her hands so she could extend them to welcome Jordan and Tilley. The couple excused the mess and explained that they were making pies for the bake sale to raise money to repair the roof of the church. Ira laughed and said that he wasn't usually trusted in the kitchen but on occasions such as this Grace would allow him to clean up while she baked.

The elderly couple graciously welcomed the two women to sit and as they all made their way to the living room Ira explained to Grace the purpose of the visit and that these two ladies needed their help. Jordan and Tilley were invited to make themselves comfortable and Ira sat down in what was obviously his favorite chair and picked up his reading glasses from the little table next to him. Grace excused herself and returned to the kitchen as Ira sat back and took a long hard look at the picture.

"Nope" he responded, "It's a mighty handsome looking family but I don't recollect seeing anybody that looks like this – maybe Gracie can help you" and he called for Grace to rejoin them. She reappeared with a tray of glasses filled with iced tea and slices of fresh baked apple pie for their guests.

Grace once again dusted off her hands on her apron so she could carefully take the picture from Ira. She slowly sat on the arm of the chair next to her husband and pondered for a moment. She said she didn't recognize the woman or children but there was something familiar about the *man* in the picture but she couldn't put her finger on what it was. She looked up at Jordan and asked if she could explain again who these people were.

Jordan had regained her composure by then and was able to relate the fact that she was the little girl in the photo and the man was her father who passed away shortly after the picture was taken.

Before she could finish; like a light had suddenly been switched on, Grace sat up straight and exclaimed "Now I remember! We bought this house from an older couple who had recently lost their son. His picture was on the mantle over their fireplace."

Ira looked confused and said, "What are you talking about Gracie?"

"Don't you remember dear? After the sale of the house was final, we found some old boxes that had been stored up in the attic. They looked like they had been up there for years and when we called to let them know that we had found them and would be happy to bring them over, they invited us for dinner to say thank you. I remember that night because that was when we found out why they decided to sell the house after letting it sit empty for so long and then they showed us pictures of their children."

Ira laughed as he removed his glasses and shock his head. "You'll have to excuse me ladies. I have trouble remembering what I had for breakfast but my Gracie can recite lessons she learned as a schoolgirl. I keep insisting that she makes up most things 'cause she knows I can't argue over what I can't remember!"

Grace gave Ira a little slap across his shoulder for his sarcasm and continued with her recollection. Pointing to Jordan's dad in the photo Grace went on to say, "This man was in one of the pictures that were on their mantle." Then Grace glanced up at Tilley and with a look of recognition she smiled and wagged a finger in the air as she said, "There was a picture of you too but you were wearing a poncho and your hair was a lot longer."

Tilley laughed and told the story of when that picture was taken - another page in the history of her colorful past that Jordan would never forget.

As they all sat laughing and getting to know one another, Jordan heard stories of her family that she had never heard before. She found out that after her dad died and she and Dalton were placed in foster care, her grandparents were left with the house. When their efforts to contact Tilley proved futile they decided to sell it. They sold all they could and gave away what they couldn't but obviously they never thought to look in the attic. It was a lot for Jordan to absorb and she wasn't quit sure what to do with all the information but it was a wonderful way to spend the afternoon. Between Tilley, Grace and Ira, the laughter, and the stories about her family, she now had a greater sense of belonging. Tilley had been her only family for so many years, but now she felt like she had a past also. She smiled as she glanced up at Tilley re-enacting specific moments of her past and remembered thinking that if she had grandparents she would want them to be just like Grace and Ira.

It was soon time for Tilley and Jordan to take their leave of this wonderful couple and their hospitality. They came away with a fresh baked apple pie, an invitation to return at any time, and the couple's prayers that Jordan would find her brother. Now she was even more determined to find Dalton, thinking that maybe there was something in those boxes that might give them a clue as to where to look next. They remembered passing a little motel on the way into town so they decided to go back and get a room. It was getting late and a hot shower and something to eat sounded like the right recipe for now.

As they relaxed in their motel room and chowed down on some burgers from the greasy spoon around the corner, they went over the events of the day and agreed that the next step would be to try and find those boxes from the attic.

Tilley's parents had passed on when Jordan was just a young girl. Jordan remembered her aunt being summoned home to make arrangements but instead of taking Jordan with her she was sent to stay with the neighbors for about a week or more. Remembering this made her think about how strange that now sounded and asked Tilley why she wouldn't let her go with her at the time, after all - they were her grandparents.

Tilley sat back in her chair and thought carefully about how she would answer. "Well . . . at the time, being a parent was still sort of new to me and I wondered how it would affect you. You were still having nightmares that you wouldn't talk about and I decided that maybe going back would be too traumatic for you. I'm sorry if you feel I made the wrong decision but it was the choice my gut made so I went with it."

Jordan was puzzled by her explanation and asked, "What do you mean the choice your *gut* made?"

"Well . . . there's only one way to make a tough choice. If the decision you make takes the knot out of your stomach then it's the right one to make. Sometimes you can't go with your heart *or* your head, you just gotta go with your gut. My head was telling me that you *should* go with me because it involved family, duty, and responsibility. At the same time, my heart was breaking with the thought that it might be upsetting for you to revisit what must be painful memories, and the battle between my head and my heart gave me knots in my stomach. Once I had decided *not* to put you through it, the knots went away so I knew I had made the right decision."

As Jordan listened, she came to the realization that she had never really appreciated what Tilley must have gone through. Without giving it another thought, she had put her life on hold for instant parenthood and never complained or made Jordan aware of any resentment. All of a sudden Jordan was feeling selfish in her quest. She was so intent on finding Dalton that she had not once considered what Tilley must be going through.

"How are you doing with all this?" Jordan asked. "Are you alright with what's happening? It must be painful for you too – after all when I lost my dad, you lost your brother, and because of me you had to go through losing your parents alone."

Tilley wiped her mouth, swallowed what was left of her burger then stared at Jordan with adoration and love in her eyes. "My sweet Jordan . . . there has never been a day that I regret having you as part of my life. If anything, I am a better person because of it. My only regret is that I couldn't find Dalton. My brother and my parents will always be a part of my soul, just like you and your brother are. Life is like a book, family makes up the spine of that book, and those you love and hold dearest are the covers to that book. Together they are always there to protect you and keep you strong. The people you meet along the way are the chapters in that book. They may have moved on or you may have moved past them, but they have been recorded and will always be there throughout your life if you ever need to turn to that experience for guidance.

Jordan swallowed a huge lump in her throat and embraced her aunt.

CHAPTER 5

The following morning the two of them decided to try to track down the boxes Grace had told them about. Tilley informed Jordan that when her parents could no longer manage being in that big house by themselves, she made arrangements for them to stay in a seniors' lodge in the city. This occurred during the time that Jordan was still in foster care and Tilley was relentlessly trying to track down the kids. She explained to Jordan how she couldn't bear to part with a lot of the memories that were in the house. After selling or donating most of the larger furniture items, she sold the house for her parents and rented a unit at a local storage facility so she could load it with boxes that she wanted to hang on to until it could be decided what to do with them. After her parents had passed she lost interest in returning to sort through them. She was still making payments for the unit and was certain that the mystery boxes had to be there . . . so off they went.

As they made their way toward the storage unit Jordan asked, "Do you still have the key?"

Tilley explained that she didn't need a key because it was a combination lock. With a crooked little smile she went on to say that she chose a combination of numbers that she was certain never to forget . . . Jordan's and Dalton's birthdays.

When they arrived at the storage facility and got out of the car, they glanced around and Tilley was the first to comment.

"Kinda creepy how so many people's lives are contained on this property yet the place seems so abandoned, isn't it?"

Jordan just nodded and took a step toward the unit and as they rolled up the large garage-like door an eerie feeling swept over both of them as they stood and stared at the contents inside. They were motionless as they took in the musty smell and looked at each other . . . no words were necessary. Tilley had already described it perfectly. It was like remnants of an abandoned life. Tilley remembered packing most of the boxes, so she suggested looking for ones that stood out or looked out of place. Before too long they came across three boxes that had different markings on them and were a slightly different shape than most of the others. When they brought them to the front and opened them they discovered that these were the ones they were looking for, so they loaded them into Jordan's car and quickly headed back to the motel.

They spent the next couple of hours eagerly sifting through the boxes. They were filled with memories of Jordan's family, locks of hair, home-made valentine and birthday cards, scrapbooks, children's drawings, baseball cards, and some photos of happier times . . . but no clues that brought them any closer to finding Dalton.

When they first opened the boxes Jordan was filled with excitement, certain that they would find something that would help in her search. A couple of hours later she was bitterly disappointed as they had hit another dead end. She *did* however take solace in knowing that *now* she had a link to her mom and dad other than just the stories that Tilley was able to tell her.

Jordan carefully went through the shoebox that was filled with pictures while Tilley quickly examined the rest of the treasures in the boxes. "There's a lot of interesting memorabilia in these other boxes, little one, are you sure you wouldn't rather go through these?" she asked Jordan.

Jordan didn't look up from the pile of photos, "No – not yet, I don't think I can deal with that right now." She just wanted to examine the photos and try to draw on the memory of each one, but there were so many she couldn't remember because she was too young when they were taken.

As she slowly replaced the contents of the boxes she couldn't help but think how Dalton would love to go through these also. With him being older, there were more memories of him here and she was certain they would mean a lot more to *him*.

They spent the rest of the day going over what they had learned so far, which wasn't much. They decided to check out of the motel in the morning and head back to the city so they could re-group and plan another course of action. Tilley also made Jordan promise that they would visit the bistro again so Gene wouldn't think they had forgotten him. They giggled as she made Jordan "pinky swear".

The next morning, Jordan loaded their luggage and the boxes into the car while Tilley insisted on taking care of the motel bill. Tilley admitted that her financial advisor had told her that she could write off expenses like this and that's why she wanted to pay the bill. Jordan just looked at her and said, "Financial advisor? We definitely need to talk . . . since when do you have a financial advisor?"

Tilley rolled her eyes like a child would when trying to play coy or pretend to be innocent of a wrong-doing and thought about starting an explanation but Jordan cut her off.

"Never mind!" Jordan interrupted while holding up "the hand". "But believe me . . . when this is all over, we *will* talk!"

Tilley made her way to the office while Jordan finished loading the car. When she was done, she pulled the car up to the office door and decided to go in to see if they sold any snacks that would be suitable for the trip. As she entered she found Tilley unloading the contents of her bag trying to find the right credit card. This was quite entertaining as the contents of Tilley's bag was very eclectic and she and the young blonde woman behind the counter were giggling as Tilley happily explained the story behind each piece as she pulled it out. Jordan stood and watched with great amusement when suddenly the young woman spotted the photo of Jordan and her family that Tilley had showed to Grace and Ira.

She carefully picked it up and said, "Oh . . . did you know Thane and his family?"

Suddenly you could hear a pin drop as the two of them stood there and stared at her, not sure if they could believe what they just heard.

The young woman was suddenly very aware of the silence and looked up and said, "Did I do something wrong?"

Taking a big gulp to clear her throat, Jordan carefully leaned toward the young woman, pointed at the picture, and as calmly as she could, asked "Do you know these people?"

While the young woman continued to examine the picture she explained, "Not all of them, but I *do* recognize the man and the little boy. The man and my uncle Ben were good friends all through high school. They were both on the football team. I understand he's since passed on but the reason I recognize him is because he's in most of the pictures that my uncle had all over his house. Every time the family gathered at their place for a holiday meal we would hear stories about the "BT Express". Ben and Thane – quarterback and receiver. Apparently they were a combination that couldn't be stopped and that was the only time our high school ever won the championship three years in a row."

Tilley and Jordan couldn't believe what they were hearing and tried to remain as calm as they could when all they really wanted to do was break out into a happy dance. They didn't want to take the time to go into details, so Tilley simply explained that Thane was her brother and they were trying to find his son, the little boy in the picture, but had lost track of him after his dad had passed away.

"Dalton!" the young woman stated emphatically.

With that, the two women found it almost impossible to remain calm as their hearts started to beat even faster. At one point Jordan could even feel her knees give out from under her and was grateful for the counter to lean on.

"Yeah – he's been back." The young woman stated. "He was a little older than he is in this picture, maybe about fifteen or sixteen but – sure, he was here for a bit. As a matter of fact when Uncle Ben found out that he was Thane's son he gave him a job in his hardware store."

The excitement was almost too much to handle. Jordan could actually hear her heart beating as she politely asked, "Is there any way we could speak to your uncle Ben?"

"I'm afraid that would be impossible." the woman replied as she put the photo back on the counter. "His hardware store ended up burning down, and after the fire

Uncle Ben took off with the insurance money and no one has heard from him since."

"Is there any way we could speak to your aunt?"

"Well . . . she's still at the house but I don't think it would be a good idea."

Tilley posed the question, "Why not?"

"After Dalton had worked at the hardware store for a short while Uncle Ben caught him stealing and ran him off. That was the night the store burned down and Dalton was nowhere to be found. No one could ever prove it but Uncle Ben was certain that Dalton set the fire to get back at him for firing him, so I'm afraid my aunt wouldn't be of any help to you 'cause she still believes that Dalton is guilty and it's all his fault that Uncle Ben took off. Truth be known though, for years there were rumors that Uncle Ben had a girlfriend but my aunt chose to ignore them and found it easier to blame Dalton for her misery. Too bad he turned out that way 'cause he seemed like such a nice kid."

Not knowing how to react to this news, the two women just thanked her for everything, paid the motel bill and returned to the car. There they sat for a few minutes trying to digest what they just heard and Jordan felt sick as a chill ran through her body.

"Well . . . *this* puts a new spin on things, doesn't it?" Tilley said.

Jordan sat in silence and stared straight ahead. She just *had* to find out more about this fire and if they couldn't talk to Ben's wife maybe she could get more information from another source. They drove to the public library and pulled up old newspaper archives. The fire had made front page news for several days and Dalton's name was implicated time and time again in the articles. Not only was he wanted for questioning about the fire, but thousands of dollars in electronics, tools, and equipment had been stolen. Jordan felt like she had just been kicked in the stomach repeatedly and couldn't find the words to respond when Tilley asked if she was alright. Even though she couldn't speak she did manage to slowly nod her head. She had just found out that her brother had turned to a life of crime. It did make sense when she thought about it, at sixteen and what must have seemed like the world against him, he probably felt like it was his only option. Who knew what else he had done while trying to survive on his own?

"Now don't be too quick to judge." Tilley tried to reassure her niece. "We don't have all the facts yet, but the good news is . . . *now* we know that he <u>did</u> come back looking for you."

Tilley was right. All they had to do now was try to figure out where he would have gone from there. With the new information, they now had a whole new set of circumstances to take into consideration when trying to determine what direction to take next. Jordan was still in a daze as they left the library so she just started the car and pulled out of the parking lot. As they made their way through town, Tilley insisted they stop at St. Augustus Church on the way explaining that she needed a land-line to make an important phone call. Jordan did as she asked and waited while Tilley ran into the church declaring that she wouldn't be long. Jordan sat there trying to comprehend what she had just learned and before she knew it Tilley was back in the passenger seat.

"OK – we can leave now." Tilley said as she closed the car door and grabbed her seat belt.

"Did you find out anything?" Jordan asked.

"Nope – nothing new, let's go home," Tilley replied as she pointed in the direction of the highway.

CHAPTER 6

They drove in silence for a short while until Tilley insisted that Jordan snap out of it and try to come up with some ideas as to where to look next. Jordan thought about it for a minute then picked up her cell phone and placed a call to another friend who worked in the office of the corrections department for the government. She gave him her brother's information and asked if he could do a search to see if Dalton was now or had ever been in the system. When he asked if there were any tattoos or birthmarks to use as a cross reference she immediately said no but then remembered to tell him about Dalton's different colored eyes. He said that would help in the search and would let her know if he found anything.

Back in the city, as they neared the main thoroughfare that took them through town, Jordan spotted the drop-in centre on the outskirts of downtown and remembered what Tilley had said about the "YMCA" and that gave her an idea.

"Where would a sixteen year old boy from a small town go if he thought he was wanted by the law and had no one to turn to?" she thought out loud.

Tilley looked at her and asked where she was going with this.

Jordan replied, "He would head for the city where he would blend in, but he would have to find a place to stay."

"The drop-in centre!" they both exclaimed at the same time.

All of a sudden things seemed hopeful again and they hammered out the facts that they had so far and agreed that they would try the drop-in centre next.

Upon arriving home they loaded the boxes and their luggage into the elevator from the underground parking and heaved a heavy sigh as the doors closed and they started their ascent. They hadn't gone far when the elevator stopped on the main floor and a pleasant looking older woman got in carrying a couple of bags of groceries.

Tilley greeted the woman with, "Well hello, Betty – how nice to see you again! How's the grand-baby?"

Jordan slowly turned her head and stared at the two of them as they carried on their conversation.

Tilley introduced Jordan and Betty apologized for not being able to shake her hand because of the bags but was delighted to meet her after all the wonderful things she had heard about her. Before they knew it the elevator stopped at Betty's floor and she stepped out saying that she hoped to see them again soon.

As they continued their ride in the elevator all Jordan could do was stare at her aunt while waiting for an explanation. Tilley seemed completely oblivious of Jordan's inquisitive gaze and just hummed along to the elevator music and watched the numbers as they counted up to their floor.

As Jordan unlocked the door and they entered the condo she couldn't contain herself anymore and blurted, "*How* do you know that woman?"

"Who . . . Betty? She rode up in the elevator with Eric and me the morning I got here. She's staying with her daughter and son-in-law for a while to help out with the new baby. They had a boy – apparently he looks just like Betty's husband."

Jordan took a minute to ask the next question – not really too sure if she wanted to hear the answer . . . "Who's Eric!?"

"I told you about him . . . he's the young man that lives down the hall . . . remember? I still say you should knock on his door and borrow a cup of sugar . . . he's single you know."

"*How* do you do that?" Jordan asked as she shook her head. "You meet someone for the first time and within two minutes you've got them telling you their life story including what they had for breakfast!"

With a sarcastic grin and an endearing look Tilley just said, "Oh now you're exaggerating little one . . . it takes more than two minutes to find out what they had for breakfast." and she disappeared into the guest room with her tote.

Once they were unpacked and settled they decided to go to the drop-in centre to see if any records had been kept that might point them in another direction. As they drove, Jordan remembered thinking how this day was much like the day she first noticed the two children crossing the street and all of a sudden she felt the same determination she did then in finding Dalton. Whatever life of crime he created didn't matter now, all that was important was finding him. In her mind she justified whatever he may have done by realizing what he had gone through, plus the fact that he was only sixteen and all alone just trying to survive. Suddenly her cell phone rang and startled her back to reality - it was her friend from corrections. She took a deep breath as she answered not knowing if she was ready for what he had to tell her.

"Sorry love . . . I'm afraid there's no record of anyone with that name or matching that description in the system." Her friend went on to explain, "I even went back another five years from the date you gave me just to be sure. You might want to try child services; someone that young might have ended up in juvenile court but the records would have been sealed. I can give you the name of someone who might be able to help you. Her name is Mary and she's been around since Moses was a kid, so if she can't help you I'm sure she knows someone who can."

Jordan asked Tilley to write down the woman's information as she drove and thanked her friend for all his help. After Jordan hung up the phone Tilley once again made an observation about her niece's personal life.

"I couldn't help but notice that you have a lot of "*friends*" that seem to be of the male persuasion and they would do anything for you - short of helping you bury a body. Are these men that you date?"

Jordan just rolled her eyes and said, "No . . . they are resources that I use from time to time when working on projects for clients."

"I see." Tilley said smugly. "Have you ever considered that maybe they would like to be *more* than resources?"

As they pulled into the parking lot of the drop-in centre, Jordan turned off the car, unbuckled her seat belt and turned in her seat to face her aunt. "I know what you're trying to do . . . stop it . . . I don't have time to date and I like my life just the way it is. Now let's go inside."

As they entered the building, Jordan couldn't help but feel grateful for the life she had compared to what she was seeing. Tilley, however, seemed unaffected by their surroundings. When Jordan made the comment that no matter how a person complained about their life things could always be worse, Tilley just rebutted with, "This is nothing compared to what I've seen in some of my travels. But you're right . . . there but for the grace of God go you or I."

They made their way to the main office and were greeted by gracious smiles from the entire staff. They once again told their story and asked if records were kept of people who stayed there. The clerk explained that signing the register was a voluntary option because *most* of their guests didn't want to be found.

"Fair enough." Jordan said and asked if there was any way of doing a search for Dalton's name. When asked for an approximate date Jordan's hopes were once again dashed as the clerk explained that the centre had only been in operation for a few years and the dates that Jordan was looking for went back to before the facility was even built.

Jordan once again felt defeated but then the clerk said, "You *could* try the youth hostel up the street. It's been around for a long time – maybe they have records."

Feeling hopeful again they gratefully took the information about the hostel and made their way back to the car. They found the address with no problem, and as they entered the office Tilley remarked on how this place reminded her of one that she had stayed at in Switzerland many years ago. They could hardly contain their excitement when they were reassured that their records went back over thirty years and details were kept of everyone who stayed there, even if it was just for the night. It only took a few minutes to do a search thanks to the use of modern technology. All their records had been converted into the computer database several years ago and with the press of a button the clerk confirmed that no one with that name had ever been registered.

As they left the hostel they remained hopeful thanks to her friend at corrections because they still had one more place to look – child services. They decided to stop for groceries before going home. Jordan would give Mary a call from there.

They pulled up to the little confectionary store around the corner from the condo and as Jordan wandered the aisles grabbing the usual perishables, Tilley went off to see if she could find the ingredients for a dish that she had learned how to make when she was in Singapore a few months back. Jordan was almost finished paying for her basket of goodies when Tilley joined her at the check-out and with great excitement looked at the little cashier and sang out, "Amanda! It's wonderful to see you again . . . how did you make out on that final exam you were cramming for?"

Again!? Jordan was flabbergasted as her aunt and the cashier discussed the young girl's future. A few minutes later the groceries were being loaded into the car by a delightful young boy sporting a smile that was completely engulfed in braces. Tilley didn't seem to know him so Jordan witnessed first-hand her aunt's gift of gab with strangers. By the time they were ready to go home she *too* knew all about this young man including what he had for breakfast.

As she buckled up her seat belt Jordan took a deep breath and said, "You have been at my side every minute since you got here . . . dare I ask how you knew that cashier?"

Tilley just grinned and said, "Where do you think I got the bagels and coffee the morning I arrived?"

They both laughed as they made their way home and Tilley made a solemn observation, "You really do have to learn to talk to people little one . . . you're missing out on a lot of wonderful experiences by walking through life with your head down."

CHAPTER 7

The two women unpacked the groceries then popped the lids on a couple of coolers and decided to relax on the terrace. As Jordan passed by her home-office she noticed she had some e-mails and realized she hadn't even thought about work for the last couple of days. She told Tilley she would join her in a minute and sat at her computer to see if there was anything pressing that needed her immediate attention. There was no new business to take care of but there were a couple of messages from some of the e-mails she had sent the night she started her search. She already knew Dalton wasn't registered with any of these agencies; Tilley's research had confirmed that, so she decided to respond to them later when she had more time and joined Tilley on the terrace. While reaching for her cell phone, Jordan asked her aunt if she still had the phone number for Mary. As she dialed she was trying to think if there was anyone else on her list of "resources" that that might be able to help. Jordan got Mary's voice mail so she briefly explained how she got her name and why she was calling. After leaving the message Jordan hung up so she could call the only other person she could think of . . . Jenny at the city morgue. Jenny was the assistant to the Medical Examiner and when Jordan worked at land titles the two of them used to party together and from time to time they would hook up and reminisce. She hated herself for thinking this way but she had to be realistic - maybe there was another reason Dalton had completely dropped off the grid. If his name couldn't be found in anyone's database, then maybe he had been found with no identification.

She knew the office was closed so she called Jenny on her cell and was delighted to actually get her and not her voice mail. She caught Jenny at home so they had a few minutes to catch up before Jordan told her the reason for her call. Jenny said, "It won't take more than a minute to do a search for the name but to search for "John Doe" over such a huge period of time would almost be impossible." Then there was a long silence before Jenny asked an obvious question. "I can't help but notice that his guy has the same last name as you – is he a relative?" Jordan had no choice but to let her friend know what she had been up to the last few days and said that this was the last place she could think to look.

Jenny thought for a moment then said, "Listen J – I can check his name for you but to look for a John Doe with no distinguishing marks other the color of his eyes would take the better part of a day so I'll make you a deal - I'll hook you up if you come down and do the search yourself."

This proposal excited Jordan. Not that she hadn't appreciated everything that her friends had done for her, but she would truly prefer to be able to do things on her own. That way she could be certain for herself that nothing had been overlooked so Jen's offer brought back renewed hope. Unfortunately, this time she was hoping that she wouldn't find anything. After all, if he was in Jen's database then that could only have one outcome – and that was unacceptable, but she had to know for sure.

The two friends chatted for a while longer then they picked a day that worked for both them and Jordan agreed to be at the M.E.'s office first thing that morning. After hanging up the phone Jordan just sat in silence. There was no need to explain to Tilley because she was right there and had heard everything. Tilley knew she had to find a distraction for her niece and with that thought she jumped up and announced that they were going out for dinner. Jordan was is no mood to argue so she just grabbed her purse and threw her phone and keys in it and obediently followed Tilley into the hallway. As she locked the door Jordan asked what Tilley felt like eating so she could recommend a place to go. Tilley smiled mischievously and said that she was going to hold Jordan to her "pinky swear" and that she would like to go see if Gene was working tonight.

Jordan hesitated and pulled back while expressing concern as her aunt tugged on her arm. "Tilley – please do not embarrass me again." Tilley put her arm around Jordan's shoulder and reassuringly stated, "Oh come now little one . . . I didn't embarrass you last time! . . . think about it . . . if *you* could control the rate of flow to the red capillaries in your cheeks you would have been just fine. *I* had nothing to do with it!"

The two of them giggled as they entered the elevator and discussed the menu at the bistro.

While they were being seated Jordan couldn't help but notice that there was no sign of Gene. As their hostess, Sarah, filled their water glasses Jordan asked if Gene was there tonight. Sarah looked around for a second then said, "He was here a minute ago – but I don't see him now. He got a phone call so he must have taken it in his office. Would you like me to ask him to join you at your table when he comes back?"

Jordan suddenly became flustered and stumbled for the words to say in order *not* to make it obvious that she asked out of interest and not out of curiosity. She tried to assure Sarah, "No – that's okay, I don't want to see him . . . I mean – not that I *don't* want to see him . . . just that I don't *need* to see him . . . I mean . . . I merely made an observation because . . . he always seems to be here and . . . never mind . . . thanks for the water".

Sarah looked a little confused but smiled as she turned and left the ladies to decide what they wanted to order. Tilley was doing everything she could to contain herself when Jordan looked her straight in the eye and said, "Don't you say a word!"

"I wasn't going to say a thing!" Tilley defended herself with a smug little smirk as she tried to stifle the giggles. "But have you given any thought to what you're *actually* going to say or do when Gene is *actually* in the room?" Then Tilley couldn't help herself any longer and broke into laughter. As she tried to catch her breath she pointed out that Jordan was not doing very well with that control thing they talked about - you know - the capillaries.

That was when Jordan lost it also and the two of them held onto their sides as they tried to suppress their giggles, but it was painfully apparent that they now had the attention of pretty much everyone in the place. Tilley is a firm believer that laughter *is* the best medicine so using her quick wit she found a way to encourage everyone to join in. She slowly leaned into the table next to them and in a soft voice that she knew could be heard several tables away she announced, "Oh you'll have to forgive us – we were discussing an ancient order of monks that just found their original scrolls and discovered that they've been spelling it wrong all these centuries – the word is "*celebrate!*"

The laughter erupted in different intervals as some of them had to have it explained to them while others got the punch line right away. Jordan was trying to catch her breath when she suddenly noticed Gene was slowly making his way to their table. As he approached, he was grinning while he surveyed his establishment with a profound look of bewilderment on his face. Apparently he *was* on the phone in his office and just came out when he heard the laughter. When he reached their table, he pulled out one of the extra chairs and for the first time sat next to Jordan.

He patiently waited while they wiped their eyes and with deep breaths managed to calm themselves before he spoke. "I get the feeling that you two are the source of all this fun and frivolity – what did I miss?"

The two of them started to giggle again and pleaded innocent, which Gene didn't believe but decided to let it go knowing that his staff would fill him later. As the three of them sat and kibitzed for a few more minutes with the usual "niceties" Jordan was grateful for the timing of the little outburst because she could use that as the reason for the rosy red cheeks she was now sprouting. While he and Tilley carried on the conversation, Jordan just stared, lost in thought and not really hearing anything they were saying. He was so nice! Why hadn't she noticed that about him? He had a wonderful personality, was easy to talk to, had a great sense of humor, and that smile . . . oh that smile! All of a sudden she was hearing Tilley's voice instead of her own thoughts and she was back in this realm, ". . . what do *you* think little one?"

"Huh . . . 'bout what?"

Tilley looked at her and said, "Where have you been? Haven't you heard a word we've been saying? I was just telling Gene about our adventures and he said that he would love to help in any way he can. Apparently, Gene here is involved with a non-profit foundation that helps people find lost relatives and wants to know if it's alright with you if he contacts them on your behalf. What do you think?

Jordan couldn't believe her ears. He selflessly gives to non-profit on top of everything else he has going for him?

". . . Jordan . . . what do you think?" Jordan suddenly snapped out of it and realized what Tilley had just told her. "You're associated with a foundation that finds people?"

"That's right. A college buddy and I started it years ago after he got nowhere looking for the family he had been separated from. The foundation has expanded in many different directions over the years; it's amazing how many people fall through the cracks of the system. We just find ways to fill in some of those cracks. I worked there for a while but shortly after my brother and I bought *this* place, he developed some health problems and I chose to work here full-time so his wife could stay home with him during his recovery." Gene turned to Jordan and smiled. "Now I'm glad I made that choice."

Jordan's gaze was locked on Gene as Tilley tried to get her attention again. "Believe me . . . I am the *last* person that wants to break this up but how soon can you contact your old college buddy Gene?"

Suddenly Gene was very aware that he and Jordan were not alone and started to stammer as he answered Tilley's question. He assured them that he was in touch with T.J. every day and would arrange a meeting as soon as possible if that's what they wanted.

Jordan pulled out one of her business cards and wrote her personal cell number on the back. She handed it to Gene and assured him he could ". . . call any time . . . day or night . . . or whenever you want to. . ."

It was all Tilley could do to restrain herself from dropping to the floor in hysterics but she had instigated this *whole* thing so she was just as much at fault.

"Well . . . I better get back to work." Gene said as he awkwardly stood up and pushed the chair back in its place. "I'll get T.J. to give you a call and let you know when he's available to meet with you. In the meantime, enjoy your dinner." And he headed back towards the bar.

Tilley looked at Jordan and said, "If you two started to talk about limpid pools of moonlight . . . I swear I was gonna gag!"

Suddenly Jordan realized that she was watching Gene walk away again and sat up and straightened her hair – as if admitting she had done something wrong.

Tilley snickered and leaned over to Jordan, "You don't have to look so guilty little one – you haven't done anything yet!"

Jordan blushed and held her menu up to her face until she felt confident that the rosy hue had left her cheeks.

CHAPTER 8

First thing the next morning, Tilley hopped in the shower while Jordan made a fresh pot of coffee. With a fresh brewed cup in hand she sat out on the terrace and so many things kept tumbling over and over in her mind. She was so focused on what she was feeling that she hadn't noticed Tilley was out of the shower and had been standing right beside her. All of a sudden she jumped when she heard Tilley clear her throat.

"Wow!" she said. "The last time someone was *that* lost in thought Sir Isaac Newton ended up with a bump on his head."

Jordan straightened herself in her chair and said "Sorry – didn't hear you come out."

"That was obvious." Tilley said as she sat and finished applying cream to her arms. "Listen little one, don't do it."

"Don't do what?"

"I know you . . . you're going to try to find a way to blame yourself for all this and I'm not going to let you do it. We can't change what has happened but we can sure take the bull by the horns from here on."

"Aw Tilley - I just don't know what to do." Jordan sighed as she sat back and threw her hands in the air. "I don't even know how to feel! I'm *angry* because my perfect little world has been shattered. I'm feeling *guilty* because I grew up with you and everything I ever needed and Dalton never experienced that. I'm *afraid* to keep looking because now I don't know what else I'm going to find out. I'm *anxious* because I don't know if he will accept me if we *do* find him. I'm *horrified* that he's a criminal – but why should that surprise me. I'm *disappointed* that he fell from the pedestal I was sure he lived on. I'm *ashamed* to admit that I even thought that maybe I should stop right now and just let things lay as they are. And you're right . . . maybe if I was a little more concerned and diligent about finding him years ago I could have changed a lot of this. I don't know! My head hurts!"

Tilley tried to console her niece with a hug but she had been through this many times in the past and knew that the only thing that would help was to get Jordan to take control of the situation and her thoughts.

"Are you going to tell me that you have no other options in your little bag of tricks?"

Jordan sat up straight and with a little sniff and a wipe of her eyes she admitted "Well . . . there is *one* other thing I thought of but it involves another road trip."

Tilley gave a little sideways grin and said, "You know how I love to travel. Tell me about it."

Well – I love the fact that my friend at corrections did what he did without question but I just can't help feeling that if I could somehow get my hands on one of their computers I could do a *different* kind of search using *different* parameters."

Tilley looked a little worried as she timidly asked "Would that even be possible?"

Jordan heaved a deep sigh and admitted "Maybe not directly but I might be able to indirectly."

"OK little one, you know I never was any good at deciphering your cryptic little mind – in english please."

A couple of years ago my friend Megan talked me into taking a cooking class with her. It was some kind of "gourmet cooking for one" and she thought it would be a great place to meet single guys. Turns out every other single female thought the same thing and the class consisted of thirteen women, one nineteen year old sous chef, and Colton."

Tilley blinked a couple of times and said "Colton?"

With a little smile in the corner of her mouth Jordan said "Yeah Colton, or Cole as we got to know him. He was our token single male and boy was he popular."

Tilley looked straight ahead as if playing a scene in her mind and shared a memory with Jordan. "You know - I remember seeing a documentary on the nature channel once which featured the feeding habits of piranhas. Was it anything like that?"

Jordan chuckled at her aunt's analogy. "Worse! Megan and I felt so sorry for the guy and for some reason I guess he could sense that *we* were no threat. Megan was looking for someone with broader shoulders and I wasn't looking at all. I think he was grateful for that so he really took a shine to us and the three of us were able to ward off the rest of the pack."

Jordan just sat and grinned while she reminisced in her mind for a couple more seconds then continued with her story. "Anyway, turned out he's the locale law enforcement of a little town just east the city. A couple of times a year Megan and I will go for a drive to take in the flavors of the town and bring him a dozen donuts."

Then Jordan turned to her aunt with a surprised happy look and waited for what she thought was sure to come – but there was no reaction. She leaned forward and slowly said, "You know – cops and their donuts?"

"Oh sweetie." Tilley said with a concerned looked on her face. "We need to work on that sense of humor of yours." Then she patted her niece's arm in an almost condescending manner and asked her to continue.

"There's not much more to tell. He always seems happy to see us and we enjoy making the trip together."

"Why was he in the cooking class in the first place? Was he there to meet women?"

"No – I think it had something to do with his mom. I'm not sure; he's so painfully shy that it was always hard to get anything out of him. He's single, is sheriff of "Mayberry", and likes donuts. That's pretty much all I know about him."

After relating her story Jordan sat for a couple of minutes to reflect on a few thoughts when all of a sudden she was aware of a deafening silence and slowly lifted her eyes to find her aunt staring at her. Eyebrows raised, head cocked to one side, and a questioning look on her face.

Oh boy, here we go again she thought. "Now what did I do?"

Tilley just shook her head in defeat and drew in a deep breath before she asked "That's *all* you know about him?" She exhaled heavily as she let her shoulders slouch. "That's so sad . . . so how is this young man going to help us?"

Well – thanks to today's technology I know for a fact that the computers for the outlaying precincts are networked with the city's main system; so I was thinking that it would probably be easier to access one of *them* than it would to get into one in the city."

"Are we talking anything *illegal* here?" Tilley's voice had a ring of concern in it.

"No. But it does mean maybe having to deceive Cole."

"Why would you have to do that?"

"In order to talk him into letting me have access to the system I'm gonna have to come up with a real good story and I haven't thought of one yet."

Tilley pondered for a moment then suggested "Why don't you try the truth? He just might surprise you." Jordan bit the corner of her bottom lip and seemed a little surprised at the concept.

"Why do you feel *you* can find something when your friend couldn't?"

"I'm not sure." Jordan explained. "I just can't help but think that if I could have access to all that information then maybe I could spot something that might ring as a possible lead."

"Like what?"

I don't know – maybe if I could get into certain data bases something might seem familiar; and if I recognize it - maybe Dalton would've also. I know it's a long shot but I would just feel better if I was able to eliminate certain things myself."

CHAPTER 9

Jordon's mind was made up and the two of them prepared for their little road trip to "Mayberry". Just as they left the city they stopped at a little bakery and Jordan ran in to buy a dozen donuts for Sheriff Cole. As they pulled up to the county building Jordan seemed a little nervous as she prepared herself before going into the Sheriff's office. Tilley sat back and seemed amazed as she watched her niece go through what was obviously a well rehearsed routine. She snickered as she compared it to the mating rituals of different species in the animal kingdom. Jordan was not amused as she adjusted the rearview mirror to apply her lipstick. Then she buttoned the top button of her blouse before flipping her hair back and Tilley voiced her observation.

"Ahh . . . aren't you supposed to *undo* that button?"

Jordan put the rearview mirror back to its proper position and explained to her aunt "Cole's not like that. He's so shy that I don't think he's even kissed a girl let alone know what to do with one if he had her. I just don't want to give him the wrong impression about me."

As she organized her purse, phone, and notes she turned to her aunt. "Now . . . I'm gonna need you to be my wingman on this."

Tilley raised her eyebrows and blinked. "Wingman?"

"Yeah. I'll make the introductions and think of something to say about why we're here. Then once I'm at the computer I need you to distract Cole so he can't see what I'm doing."

Tilley unbuckled her seat belt but remained motionless and stared straight ahead as she spoke. "I assume this means that you've decided *not* to go with the truth?"

As Jordan opened the car door to get out she hesitated for a minute then said "I'm not sure yet."

The two of them entered the sheriff's office and were greeted by a young girl asking how she could help them. An icy chill ran through Jordan as she realized that she hadn't counted on anyone else being in the office. This girl was new and Jordan wasn't sure if that would interfere with her plan . . . the plan she didn't have yet. She knew there were others that worked there but they weren't usually in the office. As she stuttered with an explanation Cole appeared in the doorway of his office and seemed delighted to see Jordan. Introductions were made and Cole ushered the two of them into his office and offered to get coffee. "I'll take my black." Jordan almost timidly said and as she placed the bag of donuts on his desk she said, "We might need it to wash these down. I got you a bag of your favorites." Then she sat back in her chair looking rather pleased with herself.

Cole just smiled as he poured coffee. "So where's Megan today?"

As Jordan reached up to accept the hot cup she explained "Oh she didn't come with us today. My aunt is visiting from out of town and I thought she might enjoy the drive plus I know how you love your donuts so it's just the two of us today."

"I see." He said as he sipped *his* hot drink. "So Tilley – are you from somewhere close by?"

Jordan glanced over to her aunt and recognized a mischievous look about her face which made her nervous.

"Actually I grew up in a town not far from here but have spent most of my life traveling. I'm just in town for a few days to visit with Jordan and see if I can tie-up some lose ends on a personal matter."

"Sounds intriguing" said Cole as he sat up straighter in his chair. "Are you able to share a little more?"

"Well it might sound a little silly but I'm at that age where a person starts thinking about one's own mortality and as I was explaining to Jordan upon my arrival; I've decided it's time to *get my house in order* you might say."

Both Jordan and Cole stared at her with very puzzled looks on their faces.

Tilley wiggled a little in her chair and continued, "Not that there is an immediate concern but with all the traveling I do you just never know when a plane might miss a runway, a ship might run aground, or a mule might miss a step on a mountain pass. Jordan and her brother are the only family I have left but unfortunately we lost track of him so many years ago when he ran away from home after his father died."

Cole seemed a little disturbed by the story and looked right at Jordan as he expressed his sincere concerns. Jordan graciously accepted his kindness but then turned her attention back to Tilley as she was dying to see where this was going.

Almost with a slight tremble of the back of her hand to her forehead Tilley continued. "I just wanted to bring the two of them together one more time before I die and know that my estate would be awarded to the two of them equally as they *are* my only living relatives. But now I don't know how that will be possible because we have no idea where he is and I have so very little left to fight with. Perhaps I should just concentrate on writing my memoires and hope that some day he might happen to read them and *then* he would know how very much he meant to me." There was almost a quiver in her voice as she finished her story.

She wasn't sure if Cole fell for the performance or not but he did seem sympathetic to her plight and asked if there was anything he could do for them to help in their search.

"Well – now that you mention it, I couldn't help but notice all the fancy technology and computers you have. Would there be any chance that Jordan might be able to look through some of those pictures that you store and maybe she would be able to recognize him."

"Do you mean mug shots?" Cole asked with a voice of concern.

"Oh nothing quite that serious – I'm sure he wouldn't be in those; but what about drivers' licenses or something? After all, we don't know what name he might be using now so the only hope would be is if Jordan could see something familiar in one of the faces."

Cole smiled and pushed his chair back so he could stand up. "I have an idea, let me see what I can arrange – I'll be right back."

As he left the room Jordan spun around in her seat and with the loudest whisper she had she said, "Are you NUTS?"

Tilley sat back and grinned as she seemed rather pleased with herself. "What – I got you in didn't I? Best of all you didn't have to fabricate a story to deceive your friend because everything I said was the truth. I just *dressed up* the delivery a little. This way if he doesn't help you he'll just figure that you have an aunt that needs stronger medication and at the same time . . . think no less of you."

Jordan was still feeling a little dishonest but as she played it all back in her mind she came to the conclusion that her aunt was right. Cole stepped halfway into his office and asked the ladies to join him in what they referred to as the "bull-pen". Tilley was quick to beg forgiveness and almost with a southern belle deployment she said, "I'm sorry dear but would you mind if I waited here in your office? It's so much more comfortable and cool. Besides; it wouldn't do any good for me to be looking, after all Jordan is the only one who would really recognize him and I'm not sure I could handle many more disappointments."

"You stay here as long as you want. I'll just see that Jordan has everything she needs and I'll be right back."

With that, Jordan rolled her eyes at Tilley and followed Cole into the bull-pen. As he helped her get settled at the computer, Jordan commented on the new faces she saw in the office.

"Yeah, we had a new sub-division go up west of town and it got a little busier around here so I finally got the help I needed with all the paper work. Now I'm free to spend more time doing what I'm supposed to outside of the office."

He helped Jordan get comfortable then explained what he had on the monitor. "What we have here is a facial recognition program. What you do is enter any indentifying features *here*, create any others that you think might apply *here*, and when you think you've created a likeness of your brother when he was a boy just press *this* button and it will age the picture incrementally until you enter the number of years or *you* stop the process. Once you have a likeness that you're happy with, just hit *this* button and it will search the DMV data base for a match. Do you think you'll be OK on your own? I'd like to keep your aunt company if it's alright with you."

Jordan was amazed and felt like a she had been handed the keys to the city. "Are you kidding? This is awesome!" Then she sat back and placed her hand on Cole's forearm as he started to walk away. "I can't thank you enough for indulging my aunt's eccentricities."

He just smiled and nodded as he returned to his office and Tilley. Once Jordan started in the program she skipped past the part she already knew the DMV had no information on. She was however, excited about the possibility of creating a likeness of Dalton and actually being able to see what he might look like today. Not wanting to take any chances of rocking the boat she closed her eyes and pictured in her mind the photo that Tilley had. Slowly she started to create a drawing from what she could remember knowing that once she could get the aged likeness, she could cross-reference it with the criminal data base. Not that she was ashamed of her brother's life-style, but without knowing what sort of a record he might have she just didn't want to risk sounding any alarms. It didn't take her long to get the process going and while the program rendered the picture she found a way into the other data bases she needed using what she called "a back door". She was thrilled that she finally had a chance to use her computer skills for something important to *her* for a change. She dated a guy for a while who was a "computer guru" and he showed her a lot of tricks to gain access to information she needed in her line of work. She was also excited at being able to access some of the files from family services. Maybe, just maybe she would be able to get a last known location before he ran away and his records sealed. She also took advantage of the fact that Tilley was working her usual magic and was able to keep Cole busy so she had the time to hack into other files she thought might be of some use. It seemed to take forever but then she realized that it was probably because she had to keep looking over her shoulder every five minutes to make sure no one was watching. She felt so self conscious and thought that for sure someone would notice the guilty look on her face and wonder what she was up to. No one seemed the least bit interested in her and she was able to go about her business uninterrupted. She remembered thinking that she would never be able to get away with this if she tried it at her other friend's location in the city. Every once in a while she would glance over to Cole's office and he and Tilley would be nattering away and laughing. She just hoped that she and Cole could still be buddies when this was all over.

All too soon she had hit all the dead ends she could handle and was no closer to finding Dalton than when she started. She closed all the files she had accessed and back-stepped to erase any proof of her being in any of them then pulled up the original program that Cole had opened for her. As she slouched back in her chair feeling defeated and hopeless she stared at the monitor and was face-to-face with a likeness of what Dalton might look like today. With her head tilted slightly sideways she realized that he was almost the spitting image of her dad. She hit the print button and returned to Cole's office.

As she entered the office the other two were winding up a conversation. They both looked up and saw the look of defeat on Jordan's face. With a sympathetic tone Tilley said "I gather you had no luck."

Jordan sat down and briefly flashed the picture she printed off and said, "No . . . but now I know what he might look like." Then she continued to stare at the picture.

An awkward silence was broken when Cole received a message through the intercom that he had an incoming call on line one.   With that, Jordan and Tilley said it was time for them to head back to the city and they thanked Cole for all he had done and they took their leave of the little Sheriff's office.

Once they were in the car they sat quietly and collected their thoughts before speaking. Jordan handed Tilley the folded piece of paper with the rendered likeness of her brother on it and started the car. As they began their trip home Tilley put her hand on Jordan's shoulder and tried to reassure her niece. "At least you know you've done everything *you* can.   Now maybe it's time to trust in other people . . . you don't have to go through this alone."

Jordan just nodded and kept driving.

Then all of a sudden Tilley gleefully offered to share the information she had learned about Cole.

"Oh . . . I should have known better than to leave the two of you alone for any length of time."

Tilley seemed a little offended by Jordan's tone and threatened not to tell if she wasn't interested. This was unacceptable as deep down inside she was dying to know what Tilley had discovered.

"Am I going to regret any of this?"

"Not at all – I think you'll find it very interesting. As a matter of fact I think you'll be down right surprised." Then Tilley sat up straight and appeared extremely disinterested as she examined her manicure while waiting for Jordan's reaction.

Jordan finally laughed and said "OK – you've got me . . . tell me all!"

 Tilley excitedly turned in her seat to face Jordan and began her tutorial. "Well . . . did you know that he has a degree in criminal science? He grew up on a farm just outside of town and moved back from the city after his father died and his mother fell ill. He spent two years in the reserves before he moved into the city. He has a black belt in three different forms of martial arts. When he came back he took the job as local law enforcer so he could spend more time with his mom. That's why he took the cooking class – he wanted to learn how to make proper meals for her because he was only used to eating fast food - like most bachelors. His mom is now in a local nursing home and he visits her everyday. He is also the local Scout Master and he doesn't eat donuts. He had a girlfriend when he lived in the city but she broke it off when he wanted to move home because she felt threatened by his relationship with his mother and tried to make him chose between them."

Jordan was stunned and out of all that she only reacted to one statement, "What do you mean he doesn't eat donuts?"

"His body is his temple and he only eats organic vegetables and does not eat pastries, sweets, or junk food. He admitted that he accepts your donuts only because they are offered as a gift and he appreciates the thought. However the *rest* of the office looks forward to your visits because they get free donuts."

Jordan looked confused but admitted "I can't believe all this. I would have thought that someone who is so painfully shy wouldn't be able to interact well enough to achieve all those things."

Tilley just smiled as she tried to explain "I hate to burst your bubble little one but the boy is about as shy and withdrawn as I am. The only reason he can't speak when he's around you is because he is completely smitten by your friend Megan. So much so that he gets flustered and starts sounding like an idiot; then he tries too hard to compensate and finds himself just shutting down before he does irreparable damage."

Jordan stared at the open road ahead. "Huh . . . I though he was interested in *me*."

CHAPTER 10

As the alarm clock announced a new day, Jordan rolled over and hit the snooze button. While she lay there trying to clear the morning fog from her head, Tilley appeared in the doorway with a cup of freshly brewed coffee for her niece.

"Come on sunshine! Time to get moving! Today's the day your friend Jenny is going to help us and you gotta get up if we want to meet her on time."

"How long have you been up?" Jordan asked as she tried to take a sip of coffee without burning her lips.

"I've been up for a while meditating and going over what Gene told us about his friend T.J. and wondering if maybe *this* is the break we've been waiting for. Besides – I hate being *scared* awake by alarm clocks."

Jordan took a few more sips of her coffee then rolled out of bed and headed for the shower. When she was done, she joined Tilley on the terrace for her second cup of coffee and told her aunt about the e-mails she received. Tilley agreed that there was probably no sense in getting excited about them at this point and she would help her follow up with them later. Besides, they didn't have time to get into them right now and they quickly got ready to make their way to the coroner's office so they wouldn't keep Jenny waiting.

When they arrived they found Jordan's friend at her desk with the necessary programs and databases pulled up on her computer and a pile of files for cross referencing if needed. After a couple of minutes of hugs and introductions, Jenny entered Dalton's name into the computer but found no record. Jordan had mixed feelings about that, on one hand that meant that her brother was hopefully still alive; but on the other hand, what if he *was* a John Doe? And if he wasn't found in *this* system, where could he possibly be? She shook her head and realized she was getting ahead of herself – first she had to eliminate her worst fear and stop over-thinking everything. Jenny showed her how to access the information and left them alone to begin their search. Jordan began entering the information in the fields that Jenny showed her and Tilley began cross-referencing the files. By lunch time they had finished another futile search, there was no record anywhere of anyone matching Dalton's description. The two were elated, but now what? They found Jenny and thanked her for all she had done. It was a huge weight off their shoulders just knowing for sure that Dalton might still be out there somewhere. Jordan promised to keep in touch and let Jen know how they made out and her thoughts went back to this college buddy Gene had told them about.

As they left the county offices Jordan checked her cell phone because she had to turn it off while she was inside. She had two messages, one from Mary and one from Gene's friend. She listened to Mary's first. Mary explained that their mutual friend at corrections had given her a heads-up so she had already started looking into juvenile records but had come up with nothing. She also explained that she was retiring soon and had turned most of her case load over to her replacement. She didn't seem to hold a lot of confidence in her new protégé's ability and left the numbers of a couple of other departments Jordan might consider trying, assuring her that she could use her name as a reference. Jordan silently smiled to herself when she recognized a couple of the departments as ones that she had already checked out while Tilley kept Cole entertained.

Jordan hung her head in disappointment as she saved Mary's message. Now their last hope lay with Gene's friend so she held her breath as she listened to the next message.

"Hi, my name is T.J. I'm a friend of Gene's and he wanted me to touch base with you concerning possibly helping you find a family member. Would you mind calling me when you get the chance so we could arrange a meeting? My number is . . ."

Jordan could hardly believe it. She let Tilley listen to the message and the two of them found themselves acting like a couple of kids – hugging and squealing.

Tilley insisted that this was a good sign; after all, Gene would never steer them wrong. Jordan didn't care about the circumstances involved – she dialed his number and held her breath again as she heard it ring.

"Hello – T.J. here."

Jordan was so excited she *almost* couldn't speak. "Hi, this is Gene's friend. I got your message and wondered if you would be available to meet with me to discuss finding my brother."

"I would be delighted." He said. "You have to understand, though, that sometimes this can be a long drawn-out process, but I've had some pretty good results in the past. I can clear my schedule for tomorrow morning if that's convenient for you?"

Jordan held onto Tilley's hand and jumped up and down without making a sound. Then she gathered herself and agreed that tomorrow would be fine. They made arrangements to meet at his office at ten o'clock. "Is there anything you would like me to bring as far as information?" Jordan asked.

"If you wouldn't mind bringing any paperwork you already have and a list of people you have contacted. That'll go a long way to saving some time so we're not duplicating any efforts that you have already made."

CHAPTER 11

As the two of them sat in the reception area of T.J.'s office the next morning, they couldn't help but notice how relaxed the atmosphere was. There were pictures of families with testimonials, abstract artwork hanging on the walls, and huge plants that someone obviously took very good care of. The whole place had a positive air about it and Tilley just sat back and absorbed every bit of it.

Without making a sound, a delightful young lady appeared. She introduced herself as Jody and invited them to follow her to an office where they were made comfortable and assured that Mr. Jefferies would join them shortly. Within a few minutes a very nice looking man entered the room and immediately extended his hand to greet them and introduce himself. He was casually dressed, yet he still looked very professional which generated an extremely welcoming "at home" feeling. As he made himself comfortable in his chair he commented on how nice it was to finally meet them because after speaking with Gene, he felt like he already knew them.

Jordan expressed her gratitude for him taking the time to see them on such short notice.

"Not at all - I'm happy to help." He replied as he turned his computer monitor to face him and began removing blank documents from the file drawers. "I have to admit that it *was* good timing on your part. I was supposed to be out of town at a seminar but a request came across my desk that required my immediate attention so I sent other members of my staff instead. I must say I'm thankful for that, otherwise I wouldn't be here to meet with you personally."

The whole environment was very relaxed and the two of them felt incredibly comfortable. He briefly went on to explain that the foundation was non-profit, but had access to resources that a lot of other agencies couldn't utilize because of government protocol and regulations. He and his staff were highly accredited and trained in almost every area required to by-pass most of the red tape "speed bumps" as he put it.

Jordan was first to state the obvious. "Gene had mentioned that you had also been separated from your family?"

"That's right," he replied. "It was during *my* search that I kept hitting brick walls manned by stuffed shirts. It didn't take long to discover that the information highway had so many restrictions that only someone from the private sector with a law degree could unlock a lot of doors without having their hands slapped at every turn."

Jordan smiled and thought about not asking her next question . . . but she just had to know. "Did you find your family?"

T.J. suddenly seemed very melancholy as he confessed, "I'm afraid I have been able to help a lot of *other* people; however . . . *my* search still continues. I haven't given up hope though; like I said, sometimes it takes longer for some than it does for others. Shall we begin?" As he smiled and turned to the computer ready to start entering information he asked his first question. "So, let's get started . . . what's your brother's name?"

Jordan gave him Dalton's information and Tilley reached into her bag and produced the photo that she had of the family.

Suddenly T.J. became very quiet and almost seemed stunned as he carefully took the picture from Tilley's hand. He sat in absolute silence staring at it. Jordan and Tilley looked at each other with great anticipation - did he recognize them?

After a few minutes he looked up at the two women before him and swallowed loudly. Then he politely asked if they could tell him again who they were *exactly* in relationship to the people in the photo. Jordan hesitated for a second then carefully leaned forward and pointed to each one in the picture and identified them. "This is my father, Thane; my mother, Rebecca; that's me on my dad's lap; and that's my brother, Dalton, standing next to our mother."

Now the situation was becoming very unnerving as he looked at Tilley and asked, "And you are . . .?"

Tilley was a little unsettled as she explained that she was Thane's sister.

He excused his behavior and considered his next question carefully, which he directed at Tilley.

"If these two children were in foster care, where were you?"

Tilley took immediate offense to his interrogation and considered not answering. "Where are you going with this inquisition? Just who do you think you are?"

He suddenly realized how forward he sounded then begged her forgiveness as he promised to explain himself if she would just answer his question.

Jordan slowly reached over and touched Tilley's hand and nodded as if silently asking her to comply. She just had a feeling that they had to follow through with this unorthodox behavior even though she couldn't explain why. She just knew that Gene would never steer them wrong and they had to trust this man.

Tilley saw the expression in Jordan's eyes and with a deep breath and a very angry tone, she began. "I have been traveling since I graduated from college. The only contact I had with my brother was at Christmas time. I would send presents for the kids that were to be given from Santa then Thane and Rebecca would send me a photo like this one to the return address on the parcel. Because I was unable to be reached when my brother died, and my parents were considered too elderly and frail, the children were placed in foster care. I spent *years* trying to locate them but was only able to find Jordan and I raised her the only way I knew how. A day has not gone by that I haven't blamed myself for not being there; if I had been, none of this would have happened. Now can you please explain to me why you found it necessary for me to defend myself to you?"

T.J. slowly and carefully placed the photo on his desk and continued staring at it for a few more seconds. While the tears started to well up in his eyes he looked up at Jordan and stated, "I can tell you *exactly* where your brother is."

Jordan didn't know how to react to those words. How could he possibly know? All he had was a photograph. Did he have something to do with him on a legal matter? Could he know him from prison? With a confused frown on her face her gaze was fixed on him as she was overcome with emotion and the tears filled her eyes also. She watched as he slowly opened his desk drawer and pulled out a small case. His hands were visibly trembling as he opened it and then proceeded to remove his contact lenses and place them in the case.

As he looked up at Jordan he revealed one hazel eye and one blue eye. He drew in a deep breath and with every ounce of strength he could find inside . . . he spoke.

"One is for daytime and one is for nighttime - that way I can always watch over you no matter what time of day it is."

It was Dalton!

CHAPTER 12

Jordan didn't even have the strength to sit up straight as her brother slowly rose from his desk and got down on one knee in front of her. He gently took her hands in his and whispered her name as he stared into her eyes. She had forgotten to breathe and found herself struggling to catch her breath. Suddenly Dalton reached up to her and the two of them held onto each other like they did when they were scared little children. Tilley's heart was breaking as she watched the two of them embrace and sob uncontrollably. Neither one of them could speak, even when they tried they didn't make any sense. After several minutes Dalton was able to stand and he gently tugged at his sister's hands to lead her to the couch behind them. Jordan's legs could barely carry her so Tilley and Dalton each took an arm and guided her to the sofa in the corner of the office. The journey seemed to be endless as she couldn't take her eyes off Dalton. Tilley poured a glass of water and encouraged Jordan to take a sip. With the cool taste of the water, Jordan began to feel better but found herself still not being able to breathe properly . . . nor could she take her eyes off Dalton.

Dalton lovingly brushed a tress of hair from her brow and softly said, "Everything's going to be alright now – I've got 'cha."

Jordan's mind was on total "shut-down" as she found herself completely overtaken by emotion. Not only could she not form an audible sentence but she couldn't even complete a single thought. She just found herself touching Dalton's face and staring into his eyes.

Suddenly Jordan was aware of Tilley's presence and slowly turned to face her aunt. Tilley was now kneeling on the floor in front of her and Dalton, and without realizing it they were both holding one of Tilley's hands.

With a smile on her lips while trying to see through a veil of tears, Jordan spoke. "We found him."

Tilley gazed at Jordan as she tried to choke back the tears and said, "Yes we did little one . . . yes we did."

What seemed like an eternity had passed before they were finally able to acknowledge what had just happened. Once Dalton was able to think clearly, he slowly released his grip on his sister and his aunt and made his way over to his desk where he pushed the button for the intercom. Without taking his eyes off Jordan he gently spoke to his assistant. "Jody – would you please cancel all my appointments, I'll be spending the rest of the day with my family."

He returned to the sofa where Tilley was now sitting and embracing Jordan. "Is there some place you would like to go to?"

Jordan broke down again as she invited him to her condo. Tilley and Dalton both agreed that Jordan was in no shape to drive so Tilley took her keys and Jordan let her without saying a word. Dalton got the address from Tilley and followed in his car.

CHAPTER 13

When they arrived at Jordan's Tilley quickly took control of the situation and led them to the terrace where the two of them sat on the gliding swing refusing to let go of each other. Tilley disappeared but soon returned with a drink for each of them. As she handed Dalton a cold beer she apologized, "I hope this is okay, I don't know about you but I know your sister needs a stiff one even if it *is* a little early in the day." As she handed Jordan her favorite on the rocks, Dalton smiled and said that it was perfect.

Jordan had been her whole life for so long but now Tilley felt like she had found the son she never knew. She had been so focused on being aware of what Jordan was going through that she hadn't prepared herself for the emotions that *she* would experience at this moment. She found herself completely not knowing how to react to what she was feeling. Tilley so desperately wanted to be a part of this reunion but thought that it wasn't her place so she fussed a little while longer until Dalton reached up and took her by the hand and asked her to sit with them so he could get to know the both of them. She was overcome by his gesture and gratefully accepted. After only a couple of sips of her drink, Jordan was finally able to think. It almost felt like she had been unconscious and was just coming to. Unfortunately now her brain was in full tilt and she had so many questions that she was making herself dizzy.

Dalton just laughed and encouraged her take a deep breath and slow down. He smiled up at Tilley and asked, "Has she always been this way?"

The three of them started to laugh as Tilley replied, "*Heck* no – you should see her when she's *really* excited."

Dalton just stared at his sister and said, "I can't wait.

Jordan stopped ranting long enough to throw her arms around him and repeat, "I can't believe it . . . I just can't believe it."

After several minutes they were able to carry on what seemed like a normal conversation but Jordan was growing impatient and wanted answers to all her questions. She wanted to know why she couldn't find any record of him ever existing. She wanted to know *everything* starting with his name . . . "Where did T.J. come from?"

"Well . . . I got into a bit of trouble when I was a kid and had to change my name so I wouldn't be found. I decided to use dad's first name and mom's maiden name: Thane Jeffries. Now everyone calls me by my initials . . . T.J."

"Was that after you ran away or after the fire at the hardware store?"

Dalton sprang back in amazement, "You know about that!?"

"Yes we do – and now that explains why you seemed to have fallen off the face of the earth, we were looking for the wrong name! Why did you run? Where did you disappear to . . . why . . . ?"

Dalton interrupted and assured her that they had lots of time and he would explain everything. Tilley volunteered to make a pot of coffee while they got started putting the pieces of their lives back together.

Jordan took a deep breath and looked her brother in the eye, "Dalton – I *need* to know what happened to you after we were separated"

As he ran his fingers through his hair he said, "Wow – it was so long ago – it almost feels like another lifetime. So much has happened since – I don't know where to start."

"I want you to start from the beginning - why did you run away?"

Tilley returned with a carafe of coffee and snacks. As she poured three cups, he began his story.

"After they took you away, I blamed myself. My heart hurt every time I thought about you having those nightmares and me not being there to rub your back so you could fall back to sleep. I had promised to take care of you and now I didn't even know where you were. I became a bit of a "problem child" and ended up bouncing around to a lot of different foster homes. When I ended up in a . . . let's say a "*not* child friendly environment", I was sick with the thought that you might be going through the same thing so I decided to take off to see if I could find you."

"Is that when you went back home?"

"You *have* done your homework." He smiled as he continued. "Not at first, I lived on the streets in the city for a while making money pan-handling and doing odd jobs like raking leafs and running errands for spare change. I was mainly focused on lying low to avoid getting caught and sent back to a foster home. After a couple of years I finally had the nerve to hitchhike back home; that was the only place I could think of to start. I guess in a way I was hoping that maybe you had been able to find your way back too. I was only sixteen so I wasn't quite thinking logically and just needed to know for sure."

"What happened when you got there? Did you look Ben up first?"

Tilley just sat and watched in amazement as Jordan asked the questions based on what they already knew and Dalton filled in the blanks.

"Not at first. I knew there was no sense in going to our old house so I thought that if I could find grandma and grandpa, maybe they could help me. When I got to their place, the house was empty and for sale so I figured the only option I had left was to check-out our old house anyway. I remember standing in the middle of the street trying to remember my way home and wondering what I would do next if I was wrong."

"Did you find it?"

"Yeah, but it was filled with another family. There was an older couple and what looked like their children and grandchildren visiting. I remember watching for a while as three little kids played in the yard and the grown-ups sat in the shade and watched. I didn't know what else to do so that's when I went into town to see if I could find dad's old school chum, Ben. Maybe he would know where our grandparents were. I remembered that he had a hardware store on Main Street so I wandered around until I found it. At the time, he was really happy to see me and when I asked about our grandparents he said he thought they had moved to a retirement home in the city. Then he asked if I had planned on staying in town 'cause he could use some help in the store and would pay me minimum wage if I wanted to stay on. I figured I might as well until I could come up with another plan."

"How did the fire start?"

Dalton was amazed that Jordan had found out so much but he continued. "It wasn't long before Ben trusted me with a key to the store so I could lock up at night. Seems he had a gambling problem and liked to spend the afternoons at the bar in the next town over where he could bet "on-line". At the time, I was sleeping in the park so once I had the key I would make a bed up every night in the back storeroom using a sleeping bag from the camping equipment we sold. I didn't have to worry about an alarm because every morning the 6:05 would come rumbling through the old stockyards and wake me up. That gave me plenty of time to tidy up and get rid of any evidence of me sleeping there. Then I would walk to the gas station down the street to clean up and grab something to eat. By the time I got back to the store, Ben would be there – none the wiser. One night a loud noise woke me up and I thought the store was being broken into so I grabbed a baseball bat and came flying out of my little corner only to find Ben standing there. He was holding a box of electronics that he was loading into his truck that was parked in the back alley. I don't know who was more scared; me or him, all I could think of was that I had been caught sleeping there. He started to yell at me and chased me out the back door. I remember tripping over a gas can as I stumbled out the door and ran down the alley. I went back to the park and stayed awake all night wondering how I could explain myself to Ben and beg his forgiveness. When I went back to the store in the morning I was surprised to see a crowd of people. The fire department was just finishing cleaning up so I stayed back in the shadows of the building next door and that's when I overheard Ben giving the police my description. Word soon got around that I had robbed the place and started the fire. All I could think of was that they will never take my word over an adult's and if they lock me up then I'll never be able to find you. That's when I knew I had to leave town. I headed back to the city and made the decision to use the name Thane Jeffries."

"So you *didn't* start the fire!?"

"No way! I found out later that Ben had run off with his girlfriend *and* the insurance money and realized that I had given him the perfect alibi for the fire. When I think about it now, he was probably setting me up from the beginning because he was pretty quick to offer me the job in the first place."

"Where did you go when you got to the city?"

"I found the youth hostel and went back to panhandling until I was lucky enough to get a job on a construction crew nearby. The crew boss took a shine to me and after a couple of weeks offered to let me stay in a little room above his garage at home. That was when my life turned around. I was able to work during the day and with the encouragement of my crew boss and his family, I went to night school and got my high school diploma. He never charged me any rent as long as I promised to stay in school and go to college when I graduated. I held a very high grade point average so I was able to attend college on a full scholarship and continued living above his garage. His son and I became best of friends and went to college together for four years."

Jordan heaved a huge sigh of relief. "I can't begin to tell you what horrible scenarios I've been creating in my mind about the life you must have been forced into. I am overjoyed and so grateful that you found the love and support of a good family. Having a best friend is something that everyone should have in their life – especially at that age." With that comment she turned to Tilley and squeezed her hand. She had always considered her aunt to be the best friend she ever had.

"Are you still in touch with your friend and his family?"

"Every day – we're like brothers. As a matter of fact . . . you know him too . . . his name is Gene." Dalton smiled as he waited for a reaction.

Jordan's mouth dropped so far that you could have driven a Mack truck through it as Tilley got up, waved her arms in the air from side to side, and did a little happy dance while singing . . . "Oh Happy Day . . . Oh Happy Day . . ."

Once again there was a lot of laughter at Jordan's expense but now she was outnumbered. Tilley was excited to realize that she now had an advocate in her corner and she and Dalton "high-fived" each other as she went back to the kitchen for treats.

Everyone used the distraction as an opportunity to relax and take a deep breath while pondering where to start next. Tilley figured that there had been too much caffeine already so she emerged with a pitcher of lemonade and some cookies that she had bought the other day while grocery shopping.

While Dalton remarked on how fresh the cookies were, Jordan's mind was still churning with unanswered questions. "What made you decide to start this foundation?" she asked as she swallowed the last bit of her cookie.

Dalton brushed the crumbs from the corners of his mouth and smiled as Tilley looked up and warned him, "You'll soon find out that Jordan *gets* what Jordan *wants* so you might as well answer now."

He sat back and sipped on his drink before he responded. "All through night school and college I hit nothing but dead ends when I tried to find you and I began to feel like I was just banging my head against a brick wall. One of my biggest problems was that I couldn't use my real name because I thought I was wanted for the fire at the store. Without being able to identify myself as a family member, I wasn't entitled to *any* information. I had to figure out a way to find you and not get caught myself. Gene came up with an ingenious plan. Instead of both of us taking business, I would switch my major and take social work and he would tutor me at night in the business courses he was taking. At the end of the term, the Dean allowed me to challenge the final business exams and I ended up with a degree in both. A background in social work made it easier for me to get into the system itself without raising suspicion. We started the foundation together; again with the support of his dad, and before we knew it we were opening doors we didn't even know existed. It didn't take long to realize that there were a lot of other families with pretty much the same story as ours, different circumstances but same story. I went back to college at night and took any course I could that might help the foundation, including pre-law, and *that* knowledge allowed me to apply for different sources of grant money for people who couldn't afford to fight the system. Now a lot of the government agencies contract our services to do background checks on small organizations who are applying for assistance. They prefer us doing it because we are also qualified to train and educate the ones who will be heading up the projects. I always made a point of accepting any contract, from the mundane to the challenging because I never knew which one might lead me to you."

CHAPTER 14

Before they knew it the entire day had flown by and they were all emotionally exhausted. They decided to go for a late-night dinner.

Tilley jumped up and proclaimed, "Ohhhh . . . I know this "cute" little bistro around the corner that I just know you're gonna love Dalton. Would you mind if we went there for a bite to eat?"

Dalton knew exactly what she was doing and happily played along, "Why, I'd love to Aunt Tallulah – do they have a dress code or am I acceptable the way I am?"

"Oh you don't have to worry about what you're wearing my dear, Jordan knows the owner and he always takes good care of her and her guests . . . I'll just get my wrap and be right with you."

"AAGGHHHH!!!" was all Jordan could come up with as they made their way to the door. "I *hate* being outnumbered!"

As they entered the bistro, the staff smiled and acknowledged Jordan but Dalton was greeted with a peck on the cheek from Sarah and handshakes from a couple of the guys. There were looks of bewilderment to see them there together but nothing was said. Dalton leaned over and quietly asked Sarah if she wouldn't mind letting Gene know he was there. Sarah happily obliged but thought it strange as "T.J." usually just went

83

right back to the office. There was a table behind a large column surrounded by plants that staff usually sat at and Dalton told Sarah that they would be sitting there tonight. As they made their way to the table, Sarah motioned for a busboy to hurry on ahead and check the table to be sure it was ready for them then she made her way back to talk to Gene.

The girls were most impressed – well Tilley was anyway. Jordan would never admit it but to be truthful, she was a little jealous . . . she always thought this was *her* bistro, yet she had never noticed this table before and it got her thinking. "What are the chances that you and Gene have been sitting *here* while I was at a *different* table at the same time?"

Dalton adjusted his chair, leaned over to Jordan and said, "Possible - but highly unlikely."

"Why's that?" Tilley asked as she scootched over to leave plenty of room for Gene.

He put his arm around Jordan's shoulder, leaned in very close, looked up at Tilley and winked, and almost in a whisper he said, "Well – 'ya see . . . my friend has been telling me for the longest time about this girl that comes in now and then and he thinks she's pretty special. So if she was here the same time I was, I'm sure my friend would have pointed her out to me . . . and I hadn't laid eyes on you before this morning."

There went the capillaries again! Jordan was so embarrassed she felt like getting up and leaving . . . that is until Gene appeared and she changed her mind.

"Ladies - It's wonderful to see you again!" he said as he nodded at Dalton who immediately stood up so they could do that male "shake hands and hug shoulder to shoulder" thing.

"I see you've met my friend T.J. – I must say it's nice to see all of you here together." He looked at Dalton and asked, "Do you think you'll be able to help these lovely ladies?"

As Tilley held a menu up to her face she smirked and mumbled under her breath, "Ohhhh . . . you don't know the half of it."

Gene was a little puzzled by her remark but turned his attention to Dalton when he asked, "Listen bud . . . I have something I'd love to share with you. Is there any way you can sit and visit for a while?"

"Sure! Just let me talk to Sarah and I'll be right back."

As Gene left them to find Sarah, Jordan put her head down and whispered to Dalton. "Does Gene know about your real name?"

"Yes. I told him and his family everything early in our friendship. They had all been so kind to me and I didn't want to deceive them so I told them all there was to tell, including the circumstances surrounding the fire. My past made no difference to them and they took me in and became my surrogate family. Ever since then, they have been behind me one hundred percent in my quest to find you. I can't wait to see the look on his face."

Gene quickly returned and sat in the chair next to Jordan, which was nicely arranged thanks to Tilley.

He sat grinning while he waited for "T.J.'s" news but soon felt uncomfortable with the silence. "You wanted to tell me something?"

Dalton sat for a moment then looked up at his friend. "I don't know how to do this or where to begin. First of all, I want to thank you for referring these amazing ladies to me. Because of *you* – *they* have changed my life."

Gene blinked and adjusted himself in his chair. "I really hope you're going to explain that statement," he said to Dalton. Then all of a sudden he noticed Dalton's eyes and spoke out loud. "You're not wearing your contacts."

"I don't have to anymore . . . Gene – I want you to meet my little sister Jordan and my Aunt Tilley."

The silence was almost deafening as he sat there staring at the three of them wondering how this could be possible. "Are you saying . . ." he stammered as he timidly pointed to Jordan.

"Yes – I'm the brother she's been looking for and she's the little sister I lost so many years ago. Tilley here is just the icing on the cake. I never imagined I would ever meet her. I found my other family today Gene, or rather they found me . . . thanks to you."

The girls once again broke into tears as Dalton and Gene embraced each other.

Gene was more excited than a teenage boy with day pass for a roller coaster. "*This* calls for a toast!" he exclaimed as he disappeared around the column and quickly returned with a bottle of his finest. He hastily poured four glasses of wine and made the first toast which was simply, "To Family".

They all raised their glasses and drank to each other.

As the rest of the evening progressed the four of them became closer, and at one point Jordan found she had removed herself from the conversation so she could sit back and observe. There was so much to share but she wasn't sure if her brain could handle too much more. Tilley was telling stories about Jordan when she was a young girl and Gene was telling embarrassing college stories about Dalton. It pleased Jordan to no end that someone else was being picked on for a change. As she sat and listened she imagined that this might be what a family dinner would be like - everyone sitting around the table sharing the day's events. She couldn't wait to get started on her new life.

They had completely lost track of all time and before they knew it Sarah appeared beside the column. Excusing herself for interrupting, she wanted Gene to know that the staff had all gone home and she would be leaving soon so all he had to do was lock up when he left. Everything was in place and ready to go for when they opened the next day and she would be in an hour early so he needn't worry about what time he arrived. She bid them all a good evening and commented on how lovely it was to see them all and hoped to see them again soon. With that she sweetly smiled and left for home.

"What a delightful young lady!" Tilley observed.

"She is remarkable and makes my life a whole lot easier," Gene commented with a sigh. "I don't know what I would do without her."

"*Oh my word*! Look at the time!" Tilley exclaimed. "If I don't get my beauty rest, who knows what this face will look like in a couple of hours?"

They all agreed that it was time to call it a night and as Gene locked the doors behind them they said their goodbyes in the parking lot. Jordan begged Dalton to stay with her and Tilley for the night. "If you're not there when I wake up – I might believe today was all a dream . . . pleeeease . . . please . . . please!"

Dalton looked at Tilley and grinned.

"I tried to tell you." She said. "That's how she got around me when she was a kid too. *You* say *no* to that face!"

Dalton looked deep into his sister's eyes and said, "Can't think of any place I would rather be. Tomorrow's Saturday anyway . . . alright . . . I'll stay."

Jordan squealed with delight and threw her arms around him, then without thinking she turned and did the same thing to Gene. As she held onto him she noticed the faint scent of his cologne and found it absolutely intoxicating, then she realized what she was doing and awkwardly backed up and apologized.

Tilley and Dalton stood side by side grinning and giving each other that *"knowing"* little look while Gene and

Jordan tried to back-peddle out of an embarrassing situation.

Gene finally got into his car and as the other three waved goodbye and watched him drive away, Jordan glanced over her shoulder and without averting her eyes from Gene said to the two of them, "*Don't* you say a word!"

"Bossy little thing isn't she?" Dalton said.

"Yeah – I blame myself." Tilley admitted.

CHAPTER 15

As Gene drove away he glanced up into his rearview mirror and saw the three of them standing there waving goodbye to him. He just couldn't help himself but he immediately envisioned them as "bobble-head dolls" as they all stood there with their arms moving back and forth with the same motion. He shifted into another gear and sped away as he tried to get that image out of his mind. While he made his way home he used the quiet time to muse over what just transpired. He and Dalton had quite a history together and now his best friend could finally come out of the closet . . . which is exactly how he would put it to him when they talked about what had happened today. He couldn't wait to share the good news with his own family. He checked his watch to confirm that it was much too late to call them tonight but then decided that maybe this was something that Dalton would rather do himself, maybe even with Jordan and Tilley there too so everyone could finally meet them.

He didn't live too far from the bistro so it didn't take him long to get home but it was time enough to let him think back on all that the two of them had shared over the years. He remembered when his dad sat them all down at the dinner table and first told them about Dalton, or T.J. as they knew him then. His dad was very concerned that the family accepted this young man. At the time, his dad couldn't tell them anything about him except that he didn't have any family and the fact that he was an excellent worker. Something about him made his dad think that T.J. had the potential to be something so much more if he could just get a break. He made a point of making everyone in his family aware that T.J. was only sixteen and chose to work hard and follow instruction instead of being a trouble-maker and shirking responsibility like so many other teens in his situation would do. His dad suggested that after dinner they all go to the garage and start doing what they could to prepare a warm living environment in hopes that it would save a young man from taking a wrong turn just because he felt there were no other options available - he wanted to give T.J. that other option. They deliberated for hours over the subject until his dad was confident that everyone was on board and in agreement so the decision could be made as a family. Over the course of the next couple of days everyone did their part in making the upstairs level of the garage livable and a few days later . . . he brought T.J. home.

Gene and Dalton were the same age and even though he agreed to the arrangement that night, deep down . . . Gene resented having Dalton there. "How come *I* can't live on my own? Why can't *I* quite school and go to work?" Being a teenager himself, all he could see was the fact that everyone was making such a fuss over this strange new kid. He was feeling like his family was ignoring him and catering too much to what would make "T.J." happy. "Don't say anything to upset T.J., don't do anything that might offend T.J., see if T.J. wants some, oh maybe T.J. would like to come along." It wasn't long before Gene and Dalton were butting heads and before he knew it, the Alpha-Male in Gene got the best of him and he confronted Dalton about moving in on his territory.

One Saturday night Gene was in the garage working on his motorcycle when Dalton came down to offer a hand. That was when Gene lost it and told him to mind his own business. They got into a heated shouting match and then Gene took a swing at Dalton but missed, which made him even madder. Dalton didn't taunt him, he just stood there and waited for Gene to make the next move. Now that Gene had showed his hand, he felt he had to follow through so he took a run at him and they ended up in a pile of tires. Dalton just wrestled him down and pinned Gene's arms to his side in a firm bear hug. Gene was getting angrier and angrier because Dalton didn't even change the expression on his face or show any kind of emotion. After a while Dalton released his grip and the two of them stood up and faced each other. After a couple minutes of yelling some more "certain obscenities", Gene took several more swings at him which Dalton simply redirected with his forearms. Every once in a while Gene would land a good one but Dalton never retaliated; he would just push him away and wait for him to come at him again. Gene was feeling pretty good about himself and was confident that he was getting the upper hand. Then he told Dalton to leave him and his family alone and stay out of his way. Dalton hadn't said a word during the whole incident, then he just simply turned and walked away returning to his little space above the garage.

Gene was triumphant; he had put "T.J." in his place and showed him who was boss. After working up quite a sweat Gene went into the house to clean up and found his dad sitting in the kitchen waiting for him. He froze in the doorway when he saw the look on his dad's face and a thousand things raced through his mind. But he was convinced that after what he just did, he could now take on his old man and anything he threw at him.

His dad stared at him for what seemed to Gene like several agonizing minutes; then pushed a chair out from under the table and motioned his son to sit down. Gene was feeling pretty cocky now so he swaggered over and joined his dad at the table. After a couple of minutes his dad spoke. "Feeling pretty good about yourself, aren't you son?"

Really going out on a limb, Gene sassed back, "What if I am?"

"When I heard all the yelling I went out to see what the commotion was and I saw what happened."

Gene leaned one arm over the back of his chair and sneered. "'Bout time someone put him in his place."

His dad was calm and spoke softly. "I wonder if you have any idea what you have just done. I don't know a lot about the boy but let me share with you what my crew-hands tell me about him. He's been living on the streets since he was twelve years old. He survived by eating out of dumpsters and defending himself against murderous gangs, thieves, and some pretty harsh elements. The guys he works with don't even *try* to mix it up with him because he has already established the fact that he could take any one of them on with one arm tied behind his back. They respect the fact that he doesn't feel the need to prove it to them. What you just demonstrated was nothing more than vanity – so who do *you* think won?"

As Gene listened to what his dad was telling him he suddenly didn't feel so invincible. "So you're saying that . . ."

"That's right son, he could've taken you down any time he wanted, but he wanted *you* to feel like you were proving a point."

His dad slowly stood up and left the room leaving Gene alone with what he hoped was something to think about. Gene was now feeling very small and even a bit ashamed; he stood up and headed for the kitchen door. As he put his hand on the doorknob he hesitated and thought for a few minutes about what he was about to do, then decided that he *had* to do it.

Dalton was sitting on his bed going over his notes for an exam he had on Monday at night school. When he heard a quiet knock he looked up to find Gene standing in his doorway looking rather sheepish.

"Was there something more you wanted to add?" He asked without making a move.

Gene stood there for a short time before asking permission to come in and talk to him. Dalton put his books down and motioned him in to take a seat at the desk across from the bed. "I just had a little chat with my dad and he enlightened me on a few of the finer points of - I guess you could say – being a man."

"Your dad's very wise; I would listen to him if I were you."

"I just found that out. What I want to know is . . . why did you let me get away with all that?"

Dalton sat up straight and leaned toward Gene while he gathered his thoughts. Then with a heavy sigh he carefully spoke. "I know you're angry, and you're angry at me. I understand that you feel I have come between you and your family but you have to believe that it was not my intention and that *I* didn't ask for this. It's not what I wanted to do and I don't know how to fix it, so I just figured you had to get it out of your system. Believe me, the last thing I want to do is cause a rift between you and your dad so if standing up to me makes you feel like you're back on top - then so be it. I don't have any family but I do remember the bond that I felt with my dad and I might have done the same thing if I felt that someone was threatening that bond."

"But you could've taken me down any time you wanted – you just stood there and took it . . . why?"

"What would getting into a fist fight have proven? That I'm stronger? Faster? That I have every intention of dividing this family and you can't do a damn thing to stop me? What good would that have done?"

Gene hung his head in shame and quietly spoke. "You have to believe me when I say that that was so out of character for me . . . I don't know what came over me and . . . I'd like the chance to make it up to you. So if you can forgive me, I could really use some help getting my bike running again if the offer still stands."

Dalton stood up and extended his hand. "There's nothing to forgive, if anything I respect you more for what you did. I probably would've done the same thing if I was feeling the way you do."

Gene accepted his gesture and shook his hand in friendship.

As the two of them shook on what would prove to be a life-long journey, Dalton added, "Besides - you punch like a girl."

From that day on the two boys became the reason Gene's dad went grey, at least that what he constantly told them. The two were now as one when it came to getting into mischief and pulling pranks but they were also the apple of his eye and he was proud to call them both his sons.

It was soon after that night that Dalton sat them all down and revealed the secrets of his past. They were all a little horrified at some of the stories he had to tell but it only reassured them that they had made the right decision when they chose to take this young man in and give him a home.

At first, Dalton only shared with Gene how badly he wanted to find his sister. It was Gene who let the rest of the family know of his search. Then it became a family quest but despite all their efforts, they could never seem to get anywhere but Dalton was relentless. For many years they would spend hours as a family talking about how they could make it happen and now, Dalton's dream had finally come true.

Now Gene was feeling a little proud of himself as he thought that maybe, just maybe he *did* play a small role it making it happen. He could kick himself when he thought that Jordan had been coming in all that time and he never realized who she was. Here he was ogling his best friend's sister and all the while . . . . ooooo . . . his best friend's little sister. Now what? He had feelings for her but how would Dalton feel about that? Should he ask his permission? He definitely had to talk to him about it. Well - maybe they'll just have to duke it out again . . . and Gene smiled to himself as he pulled up in front of his place.

CHAPTER 16

After saying goodnight to Gene in the parking lot, the other three went back to Jordan's and even though they didn't want the day to come to an end they were all exhausted so they reluctantly said their goodnights and headed for their respective rooms. Tilley had the guest room so Dalton took the futon in Jordan's office. Because of his work he never knew when he would have to make an unscheduled road trip so he always kept a light travel bag with him. It was packed with the six essentials: the three S's – shorts, socks, and shirt, as well as a pair of blue jeans, a toothbrush, and a razor. As he rooted through the bag for his toothbrush he looked around the room and noticed the little tell-tale signs that his sister spent more time sleeping here than she did in her own room. Not only were there blankets and pillows already neatly arranged for sleeping but there was also a night table with an alarm clock and a reading light. He could see her getting so caught up in her work that she would crash on the futon for a few hours then get up and continue with whatever project she was working on.

Sleep eluded him as he laid there watching the shadows dance across the ceiling in the moonlight. He couldn't help thinking how ironic it was that a person could spend years focused on one goal and then have their whole life change so drastically in the space of a ten minute conversation. He didn't like to dwell on the past, but when he had to recall those times he referred to them as the "dark years". Lying there, he found himself recapping some of the stories that had been told that night and couldn't help but go back again to what he didn't tell his sister and aunt. Especially about how he came to the realization that there was nothing he could do about his situation but at the same time knowing that he was the only one who could change it. He would never admit it to Jordan but from the time they were placed in foster care, he too had been plagued with nightmares. He didn't know how much his sister remembered but he could recall the terror *he* felt each time they were relocated to a different home and had to adjust to a new family. Not all of the homes were so terrible, but they seemed to get progressively worse each time they were moved. After they were separated, he found himself being placed in homes that would only take on disruptive children so he soon learned that he would have to adapt to the same behavior just to defend himself. He was powerless to control the thoughts that came flooding forward and he remembered the night he snuck out of his bedroom window and made a run for it. He was so terrified that he didn't even know if his feet ever touched the ground while he darted in and out of the shadows as he flew down back alleys and hid behind bushes where he would stop to catch his breath. He had thought that he left the horrors behind him but before too long he found himself in a whole new world of abuse and terror from gangs and other kinds of predators. He soon learned that even the shadows could hold certain dangers, real and imaginary.

The very thought of Jordan kept him clean and strong because he knew he would *have* to be just that if he was going to take care of her when he found her. He would avoid areas where a lot of the homeless gathered because one of the first things he learned on the run was that it was painfully apparent that at any given time any one of them would turn him in for a dollar. If he was going to make it on the streets he had to make it by himself so he quickly learned the fine art of pan-handling while trying to protect himself from the regulars who felt he was encroaching on their territory. Every once in a while he would cautiously approach storekeepers and barter for food or cash in exchange for doing odd jobs and sometimes even making deliveries on foot. Occasionally, during the winter months, he would have to take refuge at a church or homeless shelter. Those times were the scariest for him. He would try to pass himself off as older so as not to attract attention but when the lights went out, he was still just a terrified little boy. He would always try to get a cot next to a wall so he could wedge himself between the wall and the mattress. That way his back was protected and it made him feel like he had some kind of control over who he saw approaching him, but at the same time not being seen by anyone else.

The nights were always the most dangerous for him so when the weather was good, he would find dumpsters that weren't quite full and make a bed on cardboard boxes. Considering how young he was at the time it was pretty remarkable that he had already learned so much about how to survive. He figured that if the dumpsters weren't too full then they wouldn't be emptied any time soon and hopefully wouldn't be of too much interest to other scavengers and dumpster-divers. Not only were they a great source of shelter from the weather but because hunger sometimes made it impossible to use good sense they also provided the occasional meal. Most of all, it was one of the few places he felt safe.

There were many nights that he would hunker down in his metal sanctuary of trash and discards and think of all the times he had passed judgment on people who chose to live their lives in this manner. Now that the desperation of his own situation called for him to do the same thing in the name of survival, he could understand how a person could be forced into making the same choice he had because they could see no other way of making it through to the next day. In a way, this thought process made it easier for his mind not to stay in a place filled with anger, and instead he began to learn the meaning of empathy.

After he returned from his hometown knowing that he was wanted for theft and arson, he felt like he had let Jordan down somehow, blaming himself for not taking the proper precautions to protect himself from predators like Ben. He had let his guard down for a moment and now he was wanted by the law, he swore it would never happen again. His only salvation at the time came when he was old enough to hold down a proper job. Then when he was able to get on the construction crew his hopes of finding his sister made him strong again. It took a long time for him to warm up to the others that he worked with and found it difficult to trust any of them, so when his crew boss offered him a place to live he thought very carefully about it before deciding whether or not he should accept his offer. It was many months before he realized that this man and his family could be trusted, but still felt that he always had to be wary of their intentions. He finally decided that he would allow himself to remember only enough of his "dark years" to keep that balance between where he came from and being able to recognize that there *was* good out there if you were willing to take a chance. And take a chance he did, not only with Gene and his family, but also when he met Melinda.

He wished she was there. It would mean so much to be able to share all this with her, or at least even be able to talk to her about all the things going through his mind. They had been introduced a couple of years ago through mutual friends and hit it off right away. When he realized that she was going to become more that just a friend he owned-up to his past, including his real name. Admittedly, she was a little shocked at first but then she took his truthfulness as a sign of strength and admired him for having the fortitude to admit such a huge secret so early in their relationship and felt honored that he trusted her enough to tell her. As their relationship grew, Melinda recognized that one day she might have to make a choice; Dalton or her family. She was born into an aristocratic heritage that provided every her desire but it also meant that she was never in control of her own life. She often disappointed her family with her strong independent personality and butted heads with her parents every time "T.J.'s" name was mentioned. They not only disapproved of her lifestyle, which was working for a living, but they constantly argued that he was not good enough for her. To avoid their influence she had moved as far away from them as she could without actually leaving the country, but was constantly trying to win their approval. She loved them and missed them but couldn't make them understand that she had to live her own life and they would have to realize that T.J. was a part of that life. When she and Dalton talked about getting married, she just couldn't justify bringing all that emotional baggage into their lives without first trying to make it right, for Dalton's sake. She understood how important family was to him and knew that he would accept them regardless of what they thought of him. She decided to take a sabbatical and return home to try to make them accept the fact that she wanted them both – her family and Dalton. For some reason she felt she had to go through this alone and asked Dalton to be patient with her while she tried to mend the rift that had gotten so big over the years between her and her parents. She believed that the only way she could do that was if she and Dalton had no contact with each other until she was ready to give him an answer to his proposal. He knew she loved him and had faith in her so he believed she was strong enough to see this through. After all, that's one of the things he loved about her; she tackled everything with all her heart. Every once in a while he received an e-mail with nothing but a little red heart attached – her way of breaking her own rule of no contact while letting him know that she still loved him. He always responded with nothing more than "XO" – letting her know that he was still waiting for her.

With his mind racing and sleep evading him, he tossed and turned for quite some time before noticing something in Jordan's office that he missed when he looked around the first time . . . a picture of Tilley with Jordan in cap and gown, her college graduation. Not only did this make him sorrowful about missing those years with his sister but he also regretted not knowing his aunt while he was growing up.

Now a smile crept over his lips as he recalled the statement that Tilley had made in his office when she admitted to sending Christmas gifts from Santa. *Finally*! His childhood curiosity was put to rest. He was old enough to remember a couple of those years. He was at the age when he suspected that Santa and the Tooth Fairy weren't real but never said anything because of his little sister. She was very young and still believed in magic. He could still see Jordan make a bee-line for Santa's gifts and tear through the glittering wrappings like they were made of tissue paper. He had always thought that his parents did such a great job of pretending to be just as surprised as the two of them at what treasures were hidden inside, but now he realized that they truly were unaware. He had often wondered

101

about those gifts because they were always something that he thought his parents could never afford. They would always be something that was the latest craze and every kid wanted but only saw on TV. Every year he was the envy of all his friends because whatever it was - wasn't even sold in any of the stores of their sleepy little town. It almost made him believe that maybe there really was a Santa Claus.

It was a delightful part of his past that he had lost in all the darkness that seemed to dominate his memories and with his mind finally in a good space, sleep soon followed.

CHAPTER 17

The morning sun came streaming into Jordan's bedroom window and with the warmth of its rays on her face she awoke to the aroma of fresh brewed coffee. As she lazily stretched and glanced at the clock she suddenly remembered the events of the previous day and shot out of bed, grabbing her robe as she bolted into the living room. She stopped on a dime and stood in the middle of the room, staring out at the terrace. There was Dalton, standing there, looking over the view from the balcony and sipping his coffee. As he lifted the cup to his lips she could see the silhouette of the steam against the backdrop of the sky and thought to herself, what a magnificent sight! "It wasn't a dream." She said out loud.

Dalton turned when he heard her voice and smiled as he put his coffee down on the table and slowly approached his sister to reassure her. "No, it wasn't a dream."

He gently took his sister into his arms. They stood there for a moment until Jordan lifted her head and stared into his eyes. All of a sudden she was enveloped with the same sense of warmth that she felt when she was a little girl looking up at her daddy and later at her big brother.

Dalton couldn't take his eyes off Jordan either and softly asked, "Is it too early in our relationship to tell you how much I love you?"

With that comment, they both shed tears of joy but continued to hug until Tilley appeared. "That's what I like to see – siblings that *don't* fight. Maybe it was a good thing I didn't have both of you when you were growing up, I'm not sure Dalton would have survived with the two of us." She placed a pitcher of fresh squeezed orange juice on the table and looked up at Jordan. "You'd better get cleaned up little one, your brother is fixing an amazing breakfast for you and it will be ready in half an hour, so shoo . . . you've got plenty of time."

Jordan quickly had a shower and got dressed. As she tossed the clothes she was wearing the night before into the hamper she noticed a faint scent on the collar of her blouse. She realized it was the cologne that Gene was wearing and it must have rubbed off on her when she hugged him. She looked around as if to make sure no one was watching then buried her nose in it and *inhaled* deeply. When she realized what she was doing she quickly added the blouse to the heap and told herself not to be so adolescent, then continued dressing for breakfast.

As she emerged from her bedroom, Tilley and Dalton were busy setting the table. Tilley was so excited she was beside herself. "Our *first* family breakfast. Do you realize that from this day forward everything we do will be a *first*? Think of the memories we're making!"

Dalton motioned Jordan over to a chair and poured a cup of coffee for her when suddenly there was a knock at the door and Tilley gleefully opened it and let Gene in. As Tilley welcomed him with a hug, Dalton smiled down at Jordan and quietly said, "Hope you don't mind – after all, he's family too."

Okay - Jordan thought to herself; time to stop these playground antics and act like a grown-up. She smiled up at Dalton. "I can't think of anyone else I would want to share this with." With that she got up from her chair and she and Dalton went over to welcome Gene.

This whole scenario was so new to Jordan and yet it all seemed so natural. Everyone helped out in the kitchen with the final preparations and before long they were carrying everything to the table. As Gene pulled Jordan's chair out for her he leaned in closely so he could say, "I hope you don't mind my intrusion."

Jordan felt a little tingle run down her back as she caught a faint whiff of his cologne again and just for a second she was remembering the hug from last night. She looked up at him and smiled as she replied, "You're not intruding, you are *always* welcome and I'm glad you could make it."

Everyone sat down and as plates of food were passed around more stories were brought to life. Jordan was amazed at how tasty everything was and turned to her brother and said, "*You* made this?"

Dalton just smiled, albeit very humbly, and Tilley gave confirmation as she passed another full dish to Gene. "Yup, all I did was show him where everything was."

"When did you have time to cultivate culinary skills?" Jordan asked as she downed another mouthful.

Dalton and Gene looked at each other like they were trying to conceal a sacred rite of passage. Jordan and Tilley noticed the look then sat back and waited for an explanation.

Dalton swallowed his food and cleared his throat before he started the story. "When Gene and I were in college we got caught pulling a prank on a visiting football team. It's not something we're proud of now but at the time we thought it was pretty funny. Anyway, Gene's dad found out about it and punished us by making us volunteer in the kitchen at the homeless shelter every weekend for two months."

"Okay, but how does that explain how you learned to cook?" Jordan asked. "I don't think they serve meals like this at the homeless shelter."

While Dalton took another mouthful Gene continued the story. "Well, it seems that one of the other volunteers was a chef at a very prominent hotel who was impressed with the way we handled ourselves in the kitchen, so he offered to give us free lessons at a workshop he held once a week. After our punishment was done, we took him up on his offer. After all, at that time we were bottomless pits and the thought of free food was something we couldn't turn down. The rest – as you see – is history. We found out that we loved to cook. I was able to share what I learned with my other brother and soon after that we opened the bistro."

"We still tease his dad about being a soft touch when it comes to discipline." Dalton continued as he winked at Gene. "He just grumbles and says he's still trying to come up with a punishment that we won't enjoy so much."

As the light-hearted conversation and stories continued they were soon all sitting around the table enjoying their after-meal coffees and reflecting on the feast they just devoured.

While Gene helped Tilley clear the table, Jordan cuddled closer to Dalton by pacing her hand on his arm and put her head on his shoulder. As the other two returned from the kitchen and took their seats Tilley commented, "I can't tell you what it does to my heart to see the two of you together."

As Gene filled everyone's cups with fresh coffee from a carafe, Jordan looked up at Dalton and asked a question that had been on her mind and she asked it as she thought about it - but out loud. "Why weren't you able to locate me? I wouldn't think I would be that hard to find."

Dalton put his hand on hers and said, "I'm almost ashamed to admit it, but I think it was because I was trying too hard."

Jordan didn't quite know what to make of what he said so she asked, "What do you mean?"

"The absolute last thing I found out was that you had been placed permanently and once a child leaves foster care their records are sealed. I just assumed that you had been adopted so I have spent all this time trying to uncover your adopted name never once considering that your name never changed and I never in a million years would have imagined that Tilley had come back. When I was old enough I kept track of all the sites used for people who have been adopted to register in hopes of finding their birth families thinking that maybe one day, I might find your name. Even when Gene told me about you and asked if the foundation could help you, all he used to describe you was "the woman I've been telling you about"". With that Jordan looked at Gene who smiled and seemed a little embarrassed at being caught at admiring her from afar for so long. "I'm not sure he even knew your name but even if he had mentioned it, well let's just say that in my business I've come across quite a few Jordans and it probably wouldn't have stood out."

"But how can that be? I've been living here since I graduated from college."

"Think about it, little one." Tilley said. "You *live* on your blackberry, you have *no* landline only cell phones, and most everything is listed under your company name. It's almost as if you were *trying* not to be found."

Jordan saw the truth in what Tilley said and the very thought of it made her extremely sad. "You were right," she said as she looked up at her aunt, "I *have* been going through life with my head down. By trying to avoid being caught up in all the nonsense, I've not only missed

107

out on the best parts but I've also missed out on living life to its fullest. Well that stops right here and now!"

They all cleaned up and tried to plan some activities for the rest of the day. Admittedly all they really wanted to do was spend time together so it was difficult trying to think of anything else. Suddenly Tilley jumped to her feet and excitedly proclaimed that they should all go to the cabin for the weekend.

By now nothing surprised Jordan when it came to her aunt so she just heaved a sigh and asked, "What cabin?"

"Oh, I guess I forgot to mention . . . a few years ago I purchased a cabin from this delightful couple that I met in Belize. It's about an hour's drive north of here. They had decided to retire to Spain and wanted to liquidate their holdings here. They initially bought the property for their children but none of them wanted it so they sold it to me for a song and dance - literally - you should have seen my rendition of M.C. Hammer's *U Can't Touch This*." Then she followed up with a short demonstration of "hammer time". As Tilley scooted sideways left to right like a crab on a hot plate, the others killed themselves laughing. That made Tilley stop in the middle of her performance and almost looked hurt as she said, "Well we *were* at a karaoke bar."

They all agreed that it would be the perfect getaway and Tilley advised them that all they would need was a change of clothes and a sweater because the nights got cool.

With almost a shy demeanor, Jordan approached Gene and asked if he would be able to join them or did he have to get back to work.

Gene put his head down and smiled while he said, "No, Sarah gave me the day off." When he saw the expression on everyone's face he explained, "I checked in with her before I came here and when I told her what happened yesterday you'd think I had given her a raise she was so excited, so she insisted that everything was under control. She would call in extra staff for the Saturday night crowd and we will be closed tomorrow so I am *not* to show my face there or she will *fire* me. It looks like you're stuck with me."

Dalton winked at Tilley as Jordan and Gene stood face-to-face trying *not* to look at each other.

Gene and Dalton were getting ready to go to their perspective homes to pack a few things and Tilley said she would call ahead so her "people" could prepare the cabin before they arrived so all they would have to do was stop for some groceries along the way.

Everybody stopped dead in their tracks and looked at each other. Jordan was once again astounded by her aunt's remark and slowly raised her head. "Your *people*?"

As Tilley hunted through her bag for her phone book she casually looked up. "Oh yeah, I hired this sweet young couple who run the post office and gas station to keep an eye on the place. You know; keep the weeds down, mow the grass, fill the bird feeders . . . water the forest . . . just the usual stuff."

"Let me guess . . . you're doing it to help *them*."

"Well they have two little children and work so hard just trying to make ends meet so I pay them a nominal amount every month and they take care of the place for me, inside and out. Whenever I want to go out there, I just call ahead and they open it and make sure it's ready for me."

"When was the last time you were there?" Jordan asked.

"mmmm . . . about four years ago."

That remark caused them all to shake theirs heads while they resumed their preparations and Jordan wrapped her arms around her aunt. "You are *so* amazing."

CHAPTER 18

The drive up to the cabin was uneventful but enjoyable. As they made their way out of town, Jordan made note of how it was like passing through a time warp. The scenery slowly went from smog filled city streets to pristine wooded gravel roads. It was almost like entering another dimension of reality. Before they knew it they had arrived and as they entered the cabin it was obvious that Tilley's *people* had been there. The fireplace had been lit, the drapes were opened, the beds were turned down, and a potpourri of pine scented wood chips had been placed on the coffee table.

They all unloaded the car and while Tilley unpacked the groceries she instructed everyone to grab whatever room they wanted but not to take too long so they could start the barbeque for an early dinner.

After they got settled, Jordan stepped out onto the front porch and just stood in silence inhaling the fresh peacefulness of the country setting. After a few minutes Dalton joined her with two cups of home-made hot chocolate.

"Tilley thought you might enjoy this." As he handed her one of the cups they found a bench to get comfortable on. While she snuggled down close to her brother, Jordan looked up and stared at him as if she was trying to memorize every detail of his face. He looked down at her and smiled as he kissed her cheek and put his arm around her shoulder to pull her closer.

Inside the cabin Tilley was watching from the kitchen window, her heart bursting with joy at the sight of seeing them finally reunited. Gene slowly approached Tilley and with a gentle hug of her shoulders he lightly gave her a peck on the forehead and said he would go out back and chop some more firewood.

As the two reunited siblings sat motionless absorbing the clean country air, Jordan was the first to break the silence. "What was it like for you living in foster homes?"

Dalton solemnly thought for a moment while he reflected on his childhood. "Each one was different and each one got worse. Finally I ended up in one that was much like I would suspect a serpent's pit would be. They had so many foster kids come and go that they couldn't keep our names straight and would only clean up when they were going to be visited by the social worker, even then it was us kids that had to do the cleaning. There were usually three or four of us to one bedroom and the dad would lock us in; most of the time without dinner, while they went to the bar for hours on end. I would sneak out the window and jimmy the lock on the back door to get into the kitchen to get food for the younger kids. Somehow they always seemed to find out and then I would get a beating and be locked in the basement for a couple of days. I eventually found out that they were bribing the little ones with food if they would tell them who was feeding them. I had a lot of time to think while I was down in the basement. Each time I became more and more frightened that you might be in the same kind of surroundings. Then finally I realized that I couldn't help these kids but maybe I could help you if I could just find out where you were."

Jordan didn't even try to hold back the tears as she listened and then the two of them wept together.

"It's amazing that you turned out so . . . normal and well balanced considering what happened to you." she said as Dalton wiped her tears from her cheek.

"I have Gene and his family to thank for that. They're incredible people with strong family values. Gene's dad reminds me a lot of ours; hard working, honest, and believes in the golden rule. I consider myself very fortunate that they found it in their hearts to take me in and accept me as one of their own. Once Gene and I worked out a few issues we formed an instant bond with one another and that made it easier to change my outlook on life and start trusting again. Besides, if there's one thing I've learned over the years it's that life is what happens while you're feeling sorry for yourself. The way I see it – you can either choose to let the past fester inside of you like a poison or you can learn from it and move past it."

Jordan had one other question on her mind but wasn't sure how to ask it. Dalton saw the look on her face and as a little smile touched the corner of his mouth he said, "Go ahead – I know you're dying to know."

Jordan glanced down and felt a little embarrassed that she was that easy to read, but she just had to ask. "Is there someone special in your life?"

He pulled her closer and put both arms around her shoulders and thought for a moment then exhaled heavily as he spoke. "Oh Jordan, I miss her so much. Her name is Melinda and we've been seeing each other for quite some time now. On the anniversary of the first time we laughed together I asked her to marry me."

Jordan sat up straight and stared at her brother just hoping he would continue on a happier note because her heart was about to break and she didn't know what to say. He looked at her and reassured her that it was not all bad. "She has some . . . admitted issues . . . that she needs to take care of. They mostly involve her family so she said she would rather deal with them on her own and asked for some time to do so before she gave me an answer. So, I respect her decision and I'm giving her the space she asked for and pray every day that there will be room for me when she's done." Jordan relaxed a little and leaned back into his shoulder. "Don't worry," he continued. "I truly believe that we're meant to be together and she'll be back . . . it's just not knowing when and not being able to help her through this that's killing me."

"Why the anniversary of the first time you laughed?" she asked.

He put his head down and said with a smile, "That was the moment I knew I wanted to spend the rest of my life with her."

Jordan was silent for a moment and completely puzzled by Dalton's explanation. "Just how long after you met each other did it take you two to laugh together?"

Now Dalton was the one that looked embarrassed as he answered, "Ten minutes." Then his grin widened.

"Wow . . . she sounds like a remarkable woman. She's obviously had quite an affect on you. I can't wait to meet her."

"Yeah, she's pretty amazing. It's really a strange experience for me. Until I met her my life seemed so . . . ordinary, then all of a sudden being in love was so much nicer than falling in love."

They soon changed the subject back to his college days and he continued to tell her stories of Gene and his family, and as they finished their drinks Dalton made a point of sharing something else with his sister. "You know, I think my friend has a little bit of a crush on you." He smiled as he fixed his gaze on her face. "He's *good people* Jordan, and nothing would make me happier than to see the two of you get closer."

"You wouldn't think it was . . . weird? I mean, he *is* like a brother to you."

"Our relationship goes far beyond family. I'm not even sure there's a word to describe what we have. I not only trust him with my life but I would gladly give him a piece of my soul if that's what he needed." Then he squeezed her shoulder and with a crocked grin said, "So I think I can trust him with my baby sister."

After a few more minutes they decided to check on Tilley to see if she needed any help in the kitchen. Gene was just coming in the back door with an armload of firewood and Tilley was setting the ribs in a marinade she had prepared.

Gene pointed out that there was a fire pit out back and he stacked some wood next to it so they could sit out there after they ate. He also mentioned that there were some wild raspberry bushes growing next to the path that led to the stream.

Tilley popped her head up from her bowl of marinade and said, "There's a stream?"

The other three tried to contain themselves then Dalton asked if she had ever walked her property line.

"Can't say as I ever have." She admitted. "Wonder what else is out there?" She gave Jordan a container and asked her and Gene if they would pick some raspberries for dessert and let her know if they found anything else out there that she should know about.

The two of them were happy to oblige because it would be the first time they would have some time alone to get to know one another. As they strolled along the path Jordan thanked him for being so patient with her "crazy" aunt and hoped that he didn't feel like he had been railroaded into a situation he wasn't comfortable with.

"Are you kidding? I think Tilley is *great*! I can't imagine what it was like growing up with someone like her."

"It was educational, that's for sure." Jordan replied with a chuckle.

Then Jordan stopped suddenly and took Gene by the hand. "Dalton told me about how your family took him in and for that I want to thank you from the bottom of my heart. It's a tremendous relief to know that he had such a good friend to get him through the rough times. Those teenage years can determine so much about what kind of an adult a person becomes, it's a comfort to know that he had people like you and your family to guide him."

Gene smiled and they continued to hold hands as they walked. "Dalton gives us too much credit. Truth be known, it was *him* that kept *me* grounded. Don't get me wrong, we used to get into trouble every chance we got. Maybe it was because of what he had already seen by the time he came to us but he was the one that kept *me* on the straight and narrow. I'd be happy if I could be half the man he is today."

Jordan gave a proud smile and as they came upon the raspberry bushes she said, "I'm sorry to hear about your brother, is there anything I can do?"

"There's nothing anyone can do right now . . . they still haven't been able to find out what the problem is. He and I bought the bistro together but I was working with Dalton at the foundation so my brother and his wife ran it until he took ill. It's their only source of income so they talked about selling his half to Dalton to pay for the medical expenses that were stacking up. Dalton wouldn't hear of it. He called a family meeting so everyone could be aware of the situation. At first my brother was angry with Dalton but it was more out of embarrassment than anything else. That was when

Dalton reminded us of what he had learned from us as a family. He even went so far as to quote one of my dad's favorite sayings: *That the branches of a tree can survive a storm together easier than the tree trunk that stands alone.* After a couple of hours of mom's homemade cinnamon rolls and several pots of coffee, Dalton and I convinced them that the two of us could keep the bistro running so they could still have an income. I have to admit that I love being in the kitchen again and every once in a while Dalton will even ask if he can help out just to remember what it's like."

They walked and talked for quite some time until they noticed the sun was starting to set over the tops of the trees and decided they had better get back before they ran out of daylight. Jordan started to reach for the berries when Gene suddenly stopped her. As they faced each other he slowly slipped one hand around the small of her back and gently cradled the nape of her neck with the other hand, then he drew her closer. Her heart was beating so hard that she was certain she would scare away the wildlife as he softly kissed her lips and whispered, "I've never felt railroaded . . . I'm exactly where I want to be."

As they returned to the cabin they could smell the ribs barbequing, then they saw Dalton holding a beer and watching over them.

"Oh, I see you got the hard job!" Gene snickered.

Dalton laughed while he opened another beer and handed it to his friend explaining to Jordan that this was *man's* work and they were proud to do it!

"Oh *pull-eeze!*" She said and left the two of them to their "man's" work and headed inside with the raspberries.

The rest of the evening will forever be remembered as the first of many memories. There was laughter, singing around the open fire pit, amazing food, and a reassurance that all the years of sacrifices had finally paid off in different ways for each one of them.

In the morning, Jordan just lay in bed listening to the birds and enjoying the cool morning air as a slight breeze blew over her covers. It was the best sleep she had in years and for the first time, she actually enjoyed dreaming. She had to admit that it was more of a daydream as she was remembering the few stolen moments with Gene the night before.

She could have laid there all morning but was anxious to start the day with her new family. She strolled into the kitchen following the aroma of fresh coffee. There was no sign of the boys but she could tell Tilley was up by the pot of herbal tea sitting next to the coffee that was on the counter. As she poured herself a cup of coffee she noticed there was no sign of her aunt either, so she wandered the house for a minute before looking outside. She spotted Tilley in the backyard doing tai-chi exercises in her bare feet in a clearing surrounded by birch trees. Jordan didn't want to interrupt so she found a comfortable chair on the porch and just sat back and sipped her cup of morning energy while she watched her aunt with great admiration.

After several minutes, Tilley finished up and joined Jordan. Feeling revitalized she commented on how much more effective it was to exercise on terra firma and leaned over and kissed Jordan on the cheek. As she sat down and took a swallow of her herb tea, Jordan asked her something that had been on her mind for a while.

"Tilley, when we first met Dalton and you were explaining where you had been when dad died, you said something that has bothered me ever since."

"Really little one, what was that?"

"You said that you blamed yourself for what happened to Dalton and me. Is that true?"

Tilley squirmed in her chair for a moment then looked up at Jordan and confessed, "Yes, I just can't help but think that if I had been here or was easier to reach that I might have been able to make a difference in your lives."

"Tilley, you can't blame yourself for something that you had no control over. This is where you have to practice what you preach . . . everything happens for a reason."

Tilley couldn't believe what she was hearing.

"If you *had* been around and took us both in, then I never would have been blessed with the incredible life you provided for me and me alone, Dalton never would have meet Gene, you and I probably would never have this bond we have between us, but most of all . . . I wouldn't be the woman I am today. If I didn't have the scars - then I wouldn't have the love that you tended the wounds with"

Tilley was speechless for the first time Jordan could remember and the two of them held onto each other as they wept out loud.

As they backed away from their embrace Jordan said, "Besides, you're right! Dalton probably wouldn't have survived living with the two of us." The mood was a little more light-hearted as they headed back into the cabin to start breakfast.

CHAPTER 19

After getting back to the city late the night before, Monday morning seemed to come too soon. The very thought of returning to the routine of a new work week just didn't seem fair after all that had happened and Jordan wondered if anyone else felt the same. Dalton admitted that he agreed with her and could play hooky for another day but first he would have to stop by his office to see if anything pressing had come up. He reassured Jordan that his staff was quite capable of running things in his absence so he wouldn't be long and they could spend another day together if she wanted. Jordan was elated and phoned Gene to see if he could join them for breakfast before he had to go to work. Gene was almost relieved to get Jordan's call as he had been trying to figure out a way to invite himself into her day. He suggested they meet at the bistro so he could prepare a brunch for them before they opened. They cheerfully accepted his offer so after he hung up, he quickly called Sarah to let her know that they would be in early so she wouldn't be concerned when she arrived to find the kitchen being used.

They all arrived at the same time, but when they got there they were surprised to discover that Sarah had gotten there first to pre-heat the oven and grill in hopes of allowing them more time to visit before the hectic day began. Gene was extremely grateful and while Sarah seated Dalton and his family at the staff table, he started preparations for the meal. Once they were made comfortable and coffee was poured, Sarah excused herself and returned to the kitchen to help Gene.

Gene gratefully recognized what she was doing. "I can't thank you enough for this Sarah - you didn't have to do this but it means a lot that you did."

"I'm happy to help. After everything that you and T.J. have done for me, this is the least I can do. This is the best news I've had for a long time. I'm so excited for T.J. By the way, I understand that T.J. is not his true initials and he has a whole different identity . . . what do I call him now?"

As they both started to chop ingredients Gene smiled and briefly recapped the details of what had transpired then told her that T.J. would now be going by his birth name and she could call him Dalton.

As Sarah listened she remained unusually silent. After she and Gene had finished preparing the meal she helped him serve it to his new-found family then asked to speak to Gene in private for a moment. She wanted to know if it would be possible to have the rest of the day off promising to return for the supper crowd. Without hesitation Gene granted her request and suggested taking the whole day considering what she had done over the weekend. She assured him that she only needed a few hours to see to a personal matter and would return for dinner.

She watched as Gene returned to the table, and as the four of them raised their coffee cups to toast one another Sarah quietly left the bistro.

While driving home, she silently reflected on the story that Gene had told her about Dalton's family and how he and his sister were finally reunited after being separated when they were so young. She had always known that

Dalton had an unhappy childhood but he had always been very good at keeping the details of his past to himself. She had no idea of the secrets he had been keeping and she could only imagine the struggles he had endured while all the while doing so much for so many other people. Upon entering her apartment she placed her keys on the little stand next to the door and wondered if what she was thinking could possibly be true. She made her way to her bedroom where she slowly opened her closet door and reached up to the top shelf to find a box of memories that she had stored there so long ago. She carefully brought the box down and placed it on her bed, then gently opened the flaps to reveal the contents.

As things were winding down at the bistro and staff members were starting to arrive, Dalton's cell phone rang. He wouldn't have answered it except that he noticed it was from Sarah.

"Hi Sarah, is everything okay?" he asked. "Yes, as a matter of fact I'm heading to the office right now . . . I'll be there in about twenty minutes . . . I'll be sure to tell them. See you there."

This caught everyone's attention and as Dalton hung up his phone he looked a little baffled. "That was Sarah. She wants to meet with the three of us at my office."

"Did she say what it was about?" Jordan asked.

"No, she just said she needed to talk to us. Gene, did she say anything to you?"

Gene seemed a little puzzled as he tried to recall their earlier conversation in the kitchen. "She was really excited for you so I was giving her the details of what happened on Friday. Then she got sort of quiet while we were making brunch and then out of the blue she asked for some personal time. I have no idea what for – and I didn't ask."

They were soon aware that the mid-morning crowd was arriving and with Sarah not being there Gene's supervision was required so they said their goodbyes and Dalton and the girls headed off to his office.

When they arrived they found Sarah, patiently waiting in the reception area with a box on her lap. Dalton showed obvious concern. Sarah smiled and assured him that she was fine and she would explain everything to the three of them very shortly. He excused himself as he and his assistant went into his office and closed the door. While the three women waited, Sarah started the conversation by congratulating Jordan and Tilley while at the same time expressing her sincere joy. That put everyone at ease and they all began getting to know one another. Jordan and Tilley were more than happy to fill in some of the blanks and Sarah listened to both of them finishing each other sentences while they tried to put the events of the last three days into ten minutes of conversation. When Jordan told the story of Dalton's reaction to the photo, they all got teary-eyed, including Sarah. Tilley was only too happy to pull out that very photo and show it to Sarah who carefully held it by the edges as she examined it with a smile that could light the room. At one point she actually put her hand over her mouth to stifle a weepy sigh.

It wasn't long before Dalton emerged from his office and asked if they were ready to join him. As they stood up, laughing and giggling at the stories that had just been told, Sarah surprised them all by doing something very strange. Without saying a word, she reached up and removed one of the pieces of abstract art from the wall and took it into the office with her.

They made themselves comfortable at the sofa and Dalton pulled up two more chairs so they could all sit around the coffee table.

"I must say Sarah, you've piqued my curiosity," Dalton said. "Are you sure everything is alright?"

Sarah leaned the framed artwork down the outside of the sofa and smiled from ear to ear. "Things couldn't be better. First of all let me tell you how incredibly happy I am for you T. . . . I mean Dalton." With almost a laugh in her voice she said, "I'm not sure if I'll ever get used to calling you that."

Dalton put his head down and seemed a little remorseful as he apologized, "I'm sorry for the deception but it was necessary at the time – I hope you can forgive me. You can still call me T.J. if it makes you more comfortable."

Sarah smiled "I don't think so, I like *Dalton*. Gene filled me in on what happened and believe me, I understand. That's why I wanted to see the three of you, but before I start I want to tell Jordan and Tilley how you and I met." Sarah turned to face the two women as she spoke. "When I was a young girl, my father was killed in action over-seas. My mother re-married but after the wedding my step-father became violent and abusive. My mother soon turned to drugs and alcohol and it wasn't long before the courts took me away from her for my own protection. As you are aware, it's harder to place an older child in foster care so I was temporarily sent to an institution while they tried to locate my grandparents or find an appropriate home for me. Looking back on in now, I believe they forgot about me because I was there for quite some time. Shortly after I arrived, an older woman took me under her wing and watched out for me. She said I reminded her of a daughter she had lost. She had been there for a while but had incredible insight and didn't seem to belong there any more that I did. She was however heartbreakingly sad and every once in a while would tell me stories about losing her husband and children. She was an amazing woman as well as an unbelievably talented artist and would draw me pictures that would speak in ways that words couldn't. She used to say that her pictures would tell me what was in her soul because the words were too painful to speak. Shortly after we had formed what seemed like an unbreakable bond, she passed away; they said she died of a broken heart. She had no family and they knew how close we were so they gave me what little she had in the way of personal belongings. Not long after that, through their foundation, Dalton and Gene had somehow discovered I had fallen through the cracks of the system and were relentless in finding my grandparents. Even years after they reunited me with them, the two of them then became instrumental in finding the funds to put me through college. I used to think that maybe this is what it's like to have big brothers. I can't imagine where I would be right now if it wasn't for their kindness and generosity. I know for a fact that they saved my life. After I graduated I found out that Gene had bought the bistro and I applied for a job. I owe my life to these two and to the woman who painted this." As she motioned her head toward the painting she had brought into the room with her, she continued. "A lot of who I am today is because of what *she* taught me."

Now she turned to focus her attention on Dalton and slowly pulled the painting out all the way from beside the sofa, "Do you remember what I told you when I gave you this picture to hang in your office?"

"Yes I do – besides making me promise I would never get rid of it. You said "This painting would show you the future if you look close enough.""

Sarah beamed with joy and continued. "I had no idea how close to the truth that statement was. What I meant at the time was that it was the very essence of a wonderful person whose brushstrokes were the hands of time and the canvas was colored with tears of the past. At least that's how I interpreted it and I thought it would bring you luck. I can't explain it, but I just felt that it belonged here somehow."

Jordan and Tilley had been listening very intently until Jordan broke their silence. "But what does all this have to do with us?"

Sarah's eyes filled with tears of joy as she put the photo of the family down on the table, they had forgotten she still had it. She pointed to Jordan and Dalton's mother and said, "This is Becky – the woman who painted this picture."

Then she turned the picture around to reveal what was written on the back: To Sarah - with all the pieces of my heart. Love Becky.

Once again Dalton's office was the setting of intense emotion as the three of them continually touched the picture in disbelief. Tears began to flow and words were stifled with joy as Sarah sat smiling, then after several minutes she was able to continue her story. "I never put it together until Gene told me this morning about your real name. I *still* wasn't even sure when I asked you to meet with me, but when your aunt showed me this photo while we were waiting for you . . . I recognized Becky and I knew I was right. I remember Becky talking about her children and how it broke her heart not to be with them but when she remembered how she lost everything the day her husband died, the pain was even greater. That's when she would draw or paint using their love to guide her hands, that way it wasn't as heartbreaking to remember. If you look closely, you'll see your names in almost every square inch of the canvas."

Sarah handed them the painting and as they examined it more closely they could see the details that looked abstract from a distance. Sarah was right. Almost invisible to the naked eye were tiny letters all over the canvas that spelled their names: Thane, Dalton, and Jordan. From afar the clusters of letters formed different objects within the picture that made it look like just an ordinary piece of art.

"I can't explain the joy in my heart at finally being able to put this box in the proper hands – for Becky's sake." As she placed the box on the table she went on, "These are the personal belongings of your mother. Inside you will find an envelope addressed to each of you, including one to your dad. It may not seem like much but other than her undying love for you, it's all she had in the world. When Becky talked about losing her family I assumed she meant they were all dead because she never spoke about *how* she lost them. I want you and Jordan to have this." And she pushed the box toward Dalton.

Dalton couldn't bring himself to open it because he was already moved beyond words at the courage of this young woman. He chose instead to bring Sarah to her feet and embraced her. After a couple of minutes Jordan and Tilley joined in.

"This family just keeps getting bigger and bigger," Tilley remarked as they continued to hold on to each other.

CHAPTER 20

With all that had happened, Sarah found herself remembering a time that she had worked so hard over the years to forget. Her childhood hadn't always been so terrible and it was those times that she made a point of hanging on to. Her dad was a military medic with special training and had been promoted through the ranks as an instructor. This meant that they relocated at least every six months to different military bases all over the country where he would train enlisted and field operatives in basic emergency medical procedures. She was an only child and growing up as an army brat made it impossible to make or keep any friends. Because her grandfather was also in the armed forces, her grandmother understood how hard it was to form any kind of long-term bond with children her own age, so she began a tradition that she hoped would save Sarah from the loneliness of always being uprooted. Every time her family re-located, her grandma would send her a doll, one that seemed to be native to the area that she had just moved to. When they moved up north – she received an Eskimo doll, complete with fur-lined boots, the islands – a sun-tanned hula dancer, and so on. Her grandma's plan worked and it wasn't long before Sarah found herself looking forward to the moves and watching for the arrival of a new doll whenever they settled in to a new location. She would imagine that these were the new friends she would make until they had to move on again. She named each one of them and gave them an identity with their own individual personalities. Her mother often criticized her grandparents for creating an imaginary world for Sarah to live in instead of helping her come to terms with the real world.

Sarah would often lose herself in that imaginary world, especially when her parents would argue, which happened more frequently as she got older. Her mother was not happy with their life and they would often fight over when her dad would be discharged so they could settle down into a normal lifestyle. When Sarah turned thirteen her dad accepted a three month posting overseas and promised he would resign his commission when he got back. Two months into his deployment he was caught in a cross-fire between a local rebel group and some mercenaries. He died a week later from his wounds. Her mother never recovered from the loss and began living recklessly. Then they moved to a town as far away from any military base that she could find. It wasn't long before she remarried and Sarah's life was never the same.

Her mom had forbidden any contact with Sarah's grandparents so the dolls stopped coming and Sarah soon felt abandoned and alone without any new friends to help her through the transition. With her new lifestyle, her mom was soon the victim of abuse and constantly blamed Sarah's dad for all their misfortunes because she never got the chance to make it right. Very soon the police appearing at their door was a common occurrence because of complaints from neighbors, then Social Services soon intervened and felt it was best if Sarah was placed in a safer environment for her own protection. Because she had family, she was not placed in foster care, instead she was sent to an institution until her grandparents could be located. Her mom was very angry and uncooperative, therefore refused to divulge any information about their whereabouts because she didn't want Sarah to be sent to them. Since Sarah had been moved around so much, she never really got the chance to know her grandparents so all she could remember about them was that they were retired and living somewhere warm.

With her new surroundings at the facility they sent her to, Sarah recalled how her world was suddenly filled with strange people living in their own strange realities. All she had was the one doll she managed to grab before she was taken from her home, and she clung to it for dear life. Within a couple of hours of arriving at the institution, a confused middle-aged woman had cornered Sarah and started to berate her and scold her for something that made no sense. That was when Becky stepped in and proceeded to engage the woman in a conversation that made even less sense, but it made the woman turn and walk away. From that moment on Sarah was safe from the influence of her new environment and Becky became her roll model while teaching her how to survive, both physically and psychologically. Becky had shown her how to believe that there was still a place where magic could happen and dreams could still come true. She was an inspiration to Sarah and taught her that if you didn't have a dream, then there was nothing to strive for, so you have to learn to adapt and never give up hope.

Sarah used to love it when Becky would touch her cheeks and then gently push the hair from her forehead to reveal the innocence of her eyes. She remembered thinking that Becky had the perfect "mother's hands". They had the gentlest touch and just enough strength to be loving and nurturing. It was usually during these times that Becky would transcend into the other world she lived in, that place in her mind where her family was all together and happy. Those moments inevitably led to her picking up a charcoal pencil or a paint brush and begin remembering her children through her drawings.

Even though Sarah and Becky had become inseparable, Becky still found it difficult to express her feelings about her own past. So instead, they shared each other's pain by storytelling through Becky's art work. Sarah would sit for hours and listen to her hum tunes that never seemed to make any sense while she slowly and methodically depicted random occurrences from the life she used to know and express them on canvas. Many times Sarah would find it difficult to interpret the metaphors that were used in the drawings but it didn't seem to matter to Becky, she was just happy to have someone to share the tears with. It had become painfully apparent that Sarah would not be leaving this place anytime soon but as long as she had Becky, she didn't dwell on it.

They hadn't known each other for very long when Becky passed away and Sarah felt like a piece of her own identity had been taken from her. Without her friend and mentor, how would she survive? She had only experienced this type of loss one other time in her life, when her dad died. Even being taken from her mother hadn't affected her this way. She repeatedly found herself holding on to the memory of their friendship and would spend her days looking over the paintings and drawings that Becky had left her. As the next several months passed, she somehow felt empowered as she embraced the teachings that came with each illustration.

She remembered vividly the day that Dalton and Gene had come to visit the administrator of the institution. They were trying to establish a common working rapport with them through the foundation and during a tour of the facility they spotted Sarah in a corner studying the pages of one of Becky's sketch books. They apparently found it curious that someone so young could be afflicted with the same medical parameters as the other residents and would require this kind of placement. That was when they learned of Sarah's predicament and without hesitation they took action to rectify the situation. Gene and or Dalton would visit Sarah every day and within a couple of weeks, they had located her grandparents and she was well on her way to a new life. They had even arranged counseling for her, convinced that the trauma of all this would undoubtedly leave some scars. They kept in close contact with her over the years and were always aware of her progress, while at the same time developing a bond that would prove to stand the test of time.

That event had also set the groundwork for the relationship between the institution and the foundation and it wasn't long before word had spread to other agencies and organizations about the work being done by Dalton and Gene without the confines of government restrictions. To this day Dalton is notified of others who had been misplaced throughout the system due to being victims of circumstances. He and Gene even developed a job training program to help other adolescents develop work skills in order to help prepare them for independent living. Some of them were even hired at the foundation and bistro, which in time proved to be beneficial to the success of both businesses.

CHAPTER 21

As Sarah revealed more details of Becky's final months, Tilley's heart became heavy. While everyone listened, Sarah's words began to fade as Tilley could only hear the sound of her own heart beat. Even her breathing started to echo in her head as she lost focus on what was being said. She allowed herself to drift back to a time that she wasn't sure she would have survived if it hadn't been for Jordan. She had been carrying around a closely guarded secret that she was looking forward to revealing now that the children had been reunited. She was hoping that once the excitement of finding Dalton had settled, perhaps she would be able to finally reveal what she had been keeping from Jordan all these years and the three of them could finally work together in locating their mother. She hadn't considered the possibility that Rebecca would no longer be around to find. The question hadn't come up yet but she was certain it was only a matter of time. No one really knew what happened to Rebecca but it was understood that she loved her children and had provided for them in the only way she felt she could at the time.

After Thane passed away, Rebecca was so overcome with grief that she never recovered from the loss. When Tilley had finally returned home and discovered that her family had been torn apart and scattered like leaves to the four corners of the wind, her parents sat her down and did their best to explain what had happened over the past several months.

With the loss of Thane, Rebecca was showing obvious signs of prolonged grief and denial. Family Services was notified by concerned friends and neighbors who believed that Jordan and Dalton's welfare might be at risk. As with most government agencies, the right hand didn't know what the left hand was doing. Rebecca only agreed to treatment because she had been reassured by Social Services that her children were safe and being cared for by their grandparents. Yet at the same time, it had been determined by another department of Family Services that Tilley's parents were too elderly to properly care for the children so it was decided that they would be placed in foster care. Shortly after Rebecca had begun psychotherapy she requested an audience with a lawyer along with a mental health representative. She realized that this was not going to be a quick recovery and wanted to make provisions for her children while her state of mind was still considered stable enough to make those decisions. She signed custody of Jordan and Dalton over to her husband's parents and relinquished Thane's estate to them as well. Everyone involved in the transaction reassured Rebecca that she was doing the right thing and never even tried to discourage her when she also insisted that all knowledge of her whereabouts be kept secret. Only she knew the reason behind this but one can only speculate that perhaps she was trying to save her children from pursuing her out of a sense of duty in case she was not ready to be found yet, but who knows for sure. The way Rebecca's mind had rationalized it was . . . she actually envisioned herself recovering from this ordeal and when she returned home, even Thane would be there with the children.

So without ever having any contact with Rebecca to let her know what was actually happening, Tilley's parents had lost custody of the children but gained possession of the house as well as the balance of their son's estate. They were frantic and ill-advised so they weren't sure what they should do. They had spent weeks trying to contact Tilley and the stress of the situation had started to take its toll on them. Their health had started to fail and little things like decision making and thinking clearly became more and more difficult.

After several months, they had decided to sell Thane and Rebecca's house. The money was added to what was left of their son's estate and they knew they had to make arrangements for it quickly. They had originally wanted to put everything in trust for the children but social services would not cooperate in helping to make the arrangements, saying the records were sealed and therefore their hands were tied. Then they realized that it was probably for the best because there would be no way of knowing what adopted names the children would end up with so the courts would most likely have a hay-day with the funds for many years to come. They decided the best thing to do would be to put everything in Tilley's name knowing that she would do the right thing when the time came.

Once Tilley returned home and was faced with the reality of the situation, she took immediate action to try to locate Rebecca and the children. It was impossible to find Rebecca, her location had been made secret at her own request and even if anyone *did* know, no one was divulging any information on her whereabouts. Tilley wasn't too caught up in finding Rebecca at first because in the back of her mind she was thinking that eventually, she would recover and reappear. When that happened, she would be able to return with renewed strength and she would join Tilley in the search for her children.

Even Tilley had no way of knowing what had really happened, that once Rebecca had signed everything over to her in-laws, she became a burden on the system. Even with a lawyer to oversee everything, the only finances that were discussed were legal fees. She was only advised to put aside enough for short-term care for herself. Mental Health had assumed that the legalities had been seen to, including allocation of funds for her continued treatment, so once the funds were depleted and it was discovered that she was penniless she was transferred to different facilities until she landed in the one where she met Sarah.

Tilley had to use some of the money from her brother's estate to try to find Rebecca and the children because the cost of lawyers and court administration fees were piling up. Once she had located Jordan she became hopeful that Dalton was not far behind. She remembered feeling absolutely destroyed when she found out that Dalton had run away and was no longer in the system. She recalled sleepless nights where she imagined her heart being ripped from her chest and held in front of her while it was still pulsating. She tried to tell herself that she couldn't dwell on failure because she had a little girl who was also being haunted by nightmares and would need all the strength her aunt had in her if the two of them were going to survive this ordeal. In order to devote herself to Jordan, Tilley had invested more of the money from her brother's estate to hire private investigators to try to locate Rebecca and Dalton, but no matter *what* she tried the results were always the same – nothing but dead ends.

After the dust had settled and she was able to sit down and take a deep breath, she realized that when she returned home she had hit the ground running. It had been years and yet she had never given herself the time to grieve for her brother or the other losses she and her family had endured. By that time, Jordan had settled in nicely and the two of them had formed a bond that was unwavering in the face of adversity. When the overwhelming sorrow finally swept across Tilley, even though Jordan was just a young girl - she seemed to instinctively know what was happening and precisely what to do.

She didn't remember exactly when she decided to let it rest and put the remainder of the money into trust for Jordan's education, but with all that had happened over the last couple of days, it seemed like it was only yesterday. Always the optimist, Tilley had convinced herself that it had all happened for a reason and someday, they would all be together again.

Although Tilley did everything she could to hide the tears, Jordan just seemed to know, and all it would take was a touch from that little hand to immediately infuse Tilley with the strength she needed to make it through another day. This was also something that she never shared with her niece but somehow – she felt that Jordan already knew.

As Tilley returned her focus to the activity in Dalton's office, she blinked her eyes a few times to clear them then slowly became aware of the voices in the room. She experienced the same sensation she did when she comes out of a deep meditative state and is suddenly aware of the people and noises around her. She smiled to herself as she realized that no one seemed to notice that she had drifted away for a while until she glanced over at Jordan. With a knowing look and a little grin, it was as if Jordan was saying, "welcome back".

As everything that Tilley just recalled started to tumble back into place, she was grateful that her sister-in-law never knew what happened to her family. Rebecca had done what she thought was best for her children and died believing that they were being well cared for by family.

Tilley couldn't help but wonder how everyone's lives might have been different had she known the truth.

Tilley had always been waiting for the right time to tell Jordan all this, and in a way she was relieved that they had encountered Sarah before she had the opportunity to tell the kids about their mother. She couldn't imagine the devastation it would have caused to get their hopes up only to discover that they were years too late.

She even imagined that Dalton was going to hold some sort of remorse now that he had learned that he was only a matter of weeks too late from discovering his mother on his own. If only he had been at the institution a few months earlier he may have discovered Sarah sooner which may have led him to his mother and perhaps . . . but then again Sarah might not have been sitting in plain sight . . . or the two of them may have been tucked away in Rebecca's room. Well there *is* one thing Tilley had learned over the years . . . there's just no sense in trying to second guess fate. If it was meant to be, it would have happened. You could make yourself crazy with all the "What ifs".

CHAPTER 22

Dalton cleared his schedule for the rest of the day and he and his "ladies" left his office and headed back to the bistro to share the good news with Gene. As they were driving, Jordan remembered to tell Dalton about the three boxes they had found when they went home.

"Now *there's* a story I want to hear about," he said and as they drove on and the two of them tried to give him the abbreviated version.

"Sounds like this Grace and Ira were the older couple that I remember seeing when I went home. Does Ira use a cane?"

The girls laughed and said that they couldn't wait to see their faces when they went back for some more apple pie and showed up with Dalton.

"That reminds me, little one . . . first thing tomorrow you should phone your friends and let them know how things have turned out." Tilley said to Jordan as they pulled up to the bistro.

"You're right, especially Jen. She'll be so happy to know that I found my "John Doe"." She said as she patted Dalton on the shoulder and grinned.

Dalton looked at Jordan with great bewilderment and said, "Do I *want* to know what you're talking about?" The two women snickered with each other as they all entered the bistro.

As Gene greeted them, Sarah emphatically said she would take over from here so Gene could sit and visit. She quickly hurried them off to the special table behind the column of foliage and insisted that Gene take a break. "I think Dalton has something to tell you." and she winked at him as she left.

"Don't keep me in suspense any longer. What happened?"

Over the next several minutes the three of them tried to put the events in perspective as they told Gene about Sarah's relationship with their mother and the box that she gave them. He was mesmerized as he tried to listen to all three of them talk at once and eventually he was able to get the whole story.

"This just keeps getting better and better. I wonder what *else* could happen to make this more perfect." he said.

Tilley agreed. "Well, anything is possible. After all - things *do* happen in threes 'ya know. Besides, you can't fight destiny."

Jordan acknowledged her aunt's statement with, "Here we go again," then turned to Dalton and explained. "Our aunt is a great believer in destiny and everything happening for a reason."

Dalton smiled at her and said, "I gather you don't share that belief?"

"Call me a cynic, but I have trouble with believing that some *greater force* has pre-determined what the future holds in store for us. That would be like admitting that you're blindly following someone else's preconceived idea of what you should do and if there's one thing I hate it's . . ."

". . . being told what to do!" Dalton and Tilley laughed as they finished the sentence for her in unison.

"You see what I have to put up with now?" Jordan exclaimed as she turned to Gene.

The laughter continued as they celebrated, and before they knew it the afternoon had quickly passed so they decided to return to Jordan's for the evening. They agreed that they felt they were ready to go through the contents of the box that Sarah had presented to them and maybe even the ones that Jordan and Tilley had found. Jordan admitted that she couldn't remember much about what was in them because she wasn't in the right frame of mind at the time and wouldn't mind going through them again.

"Maybe it's because you were *meant* to go through them together." Tilley smugly commented as she rolled her eyes upward.

Everyone chuckled as it was an obvious dig at Jordan.

Dalton turned to Gene. "If I remember correctly, dinnertime on Monday is pretty slow around here and it would mean a lot to me if you could join us this evening."

Gene wasn't sure how to respond. "I'd hate to intrude on such an intimate family moment," he said as he turned to Jordan.

Jordan shyly smiled and reassured him that he was a huge part of this family now and it would also mean a lot to her if he could be there.

He accepted and as they got up to leave, Gene said he had to go over a few things with Sarah before he left and would catch up with them at Jordan's.

CHAPTER 23

Back at the condo, the three of them were gathering the boxes in one place while at the same time settling down with a cool drink when the buzzer for the door announced Gene's arrival. As he entered, he presented them with containers of take-out and two bottles of wine. "I come bearing gifts - I hope you don't mind but I thought it might be nice if nobody had to cook." Tilley turned the TV to a music video station for some background entertainment while they sat down to enjoy their evening meal together.

They were about half way through when Dalton suddenly pointed to the television and excitedly asked Jordan to turn up the volume. As she ran to find the remote control, Dalton almost choked on a mouthful of food as he shouted, "That's Ben!"

The hourly news break was on and as Jordan increased the volume, they all gathered around the TV just in time to see a news report with a man being led in handcuffs to a police cruiser. He had been arrested by the Las Vegas police on charges of arson and insurance fraud. He was charged with setting fire to an adult video store that he owned in order to collect the insurance to pay off gambling debts. The insurance company said they would be re-opening investigations into suspicious circumstances surrounding three other claims that other

141

insurance companies have paid out over the past several years for similar fires at a hardware store, laundromat, and a newsstand that the accused also owned.

Dalton just erupted with laughter as he pointed to his head, "Note to self . . . contact insurance company and clear name."

"Are you sure that's wise?" Jordan asked, "What if they don't believe you and . . . ."

Dalton stopped her from continuing and assured her that the statute of limitations has run out, and with his legal background he knew just what to do.

They all raised their glasses in celebration and continued to feast while feeling rather gratified that Dalton's past was no longer a "shady" one.

When they were finished, Dalton admitted that he was now eager to get started on the boxes so they made themselves comfortable in the living room and with a deep breath, Jordan reached for the box that Sarah had given them. It was at this time that Tilley chose to disclose the secret that she had kept so closely to her heart all these years. When she finished, she begged Jordan's forgiveness for not telling her sooner.

Jordan and Dalton were stunned by this new development. Dalton admitted that he had often thought about his mother but in a very different light. Always wondering why she had let this happen to them but never really sure if he was ready for the truth. He was comfortable with the story that Sarah had related to them because for an instant, it felt a little like closure. Jordan's heart was breaking as she witnessed her aunt, who was obviously finding it painful, try to search out the right words to properly disclose the facts in a way that would avoid her and her brother from being too judgmental toward their mother.

The two of them sat holding each other's hand as they listened to Tilley. For the first time, they felt a mixture of emotions toward their mother: sorrow, regret, and yet at the same time, on some level, admiration and excitement. They finally had the answer they had been waiting for so long to hear, that their mother hadn't intentionally abandoned them.

Jordan and Dalton sat and stared at the box for a couple of minutes until Dalton gathered the nerve to be the first to open it. They weren't sure what to expect; all they knew was that this was their mother's legacy which was something they never dreamed of sharing but now looked forward to.

As they pulled out little mementos one at a time they tried to imagine exactly what these things might have meant to their mother. Then they discovered a sketch book on the bottom of the box and as they flipped through the pages, it was almost like witnessing a visual tutorial of their mother's life. They had no idea that she was so incredibly talented as an artist. But it was the obvious torment she was in that broke their hearts. Every picture revealed her pain and at the same time demonstrated the love she still held for her children, plus the guilt she felt for not having the courage to be with them.

Neatly tucked between the pages, they found the envelopes that Sarah had mentioned. Jordan carefully took the one addressed to her and held it close to her heart, admitting that she wasn't ready to open it yet. Dalton agreed as he put his in his pocket. They decided to read them in private when the time was right and would only read the one addressed to their dad when the two of them had given it more thought.

As they reached for the other three boxes they suddenly heard a musical lament of Steppenwolf's "*Born to Be Wild*". Tilley jumped up and apologized as she fumbled to find her cell phone in the bottom of her bag.

The distraction broke the strain of the solemn mood and as she rummaged through her bag trying to find her phone, the other three looked at each other for a moment but none of them dared say anything.

"How befitting!" Jordan remarked while the giggles started.

Tilley ran off to another room to take the call so the others used that time to reflect on everything that had happened.

As they sat in conversation and chuckled at Tilley's choice of ring tones, they hadn't noticed that she had reappeared with an almost ominous look on her face. Startled, they all looked up at her.

She couldn't speak as she stood holding her phone in her hand when suddenly her look changed from foreboding to absolute joy.

The other three were completely baffled as Dalton asked, "Tilley, is everything alright . . . are you okay?"

She stood motionless starring at her phone for a few more seconds before dropping it on the sofa as if it had scorched her hand then ran toward the kitchen flapping her arms and exclaiming, "I need a drink!" She quickly emerged from the kitchen with four glasses and the two bottles of wine that Gene had brought.

As she poured one for everybody she spoke with a very shaky voice. "Trust me, you're gonna *want* a drink when I tell you what I just found out!"

She downed her wine without taking a breath then poured herself another one.

As entertaining as this was, the other three were indescribably intrigued and the suspense was killing them.

Jordan reached for her aunt, "Tilley! Just take a deep breath and tell us who was on the phone."

When she tried to speak she sounded like the Swedish Chef trying to give a dissertation in Yiddish. The others could hardly contain themselves, so while trying not to laugh out loud they did their best to get her to calm down so they could understand what she was trying to say. She once again downed another glass of wine and *that* one seemed to do the trick as she relaxed enough to sit back and breathe.

She held up one hand and assured them that she was okay now and then began. First she turned to Gene, "Do you remember saying you wondered how this could get any better? Well hang on to your Hanes baby-cakes 'cause here comes number three and it's a doosy!"

She heaved a huge sigh and started. "I hope you don't mind little one but I couldn't sleep one night and when meditation didn't work I got up to look for something to pass the time with and ended up going through these boxes again. I just wanted to remember my brother in my own space without causing you any more pain than you had already been through. I found a couple of things of interest so I put a call into my financial advisor." She leaned forward and looked right at Jordan and reiterated "*Yes* my financial advisor! - I was curious to know if any of them were worth anything today"

"Well, that was him on the phone and you're *not* gonna believe what he just told me." She leaned back and pointed to one of the boxes. "It seems that on the day that both of you were born your father purchased shares in different companies in each of your names. You'll find them in an envelope taped to the back page of the orange scrapbook in *that* box. There are also unopened packages of baseball and football cards in a cigar box."

Jordan and Dalton looked at each other inquisitively as they slowly opened the box she was pointing to and removed the scrapbook and the cigar box.

She took a long deep breath before continuing. "Apparently . . . between the shares and the unopened rookie cards . . ."

Tilley shook her head, blinked several times, took another drink, and finished with . . . "You kids are wealthier than you ever could imagine!"

There was nothing but silence as Tilley slouched back on the sofa and inhaled the rest of her third glass of wine, then stared straight ahead as if she had been hypnotized.

Jordan and Dalton turned to each other and then one opened the cigar box as the other found the envelope in the scrapbook. After several minutes of sitting in silent disbelief the celebration erupted!

CHAPTER 24

Still trying to wrap their heads around what just happened, the four of them poured more wine and carefully perused the documents they were holding. Jordan was certain the neighbors would have called the police because of the racket they were making but it wasn't long before they were able to settle down and catch their breath.

On each of their birthdays their dad has purchased shares in two companies, all four of these companies were now multi-million dollar corporations and it was mind-boggling to try to imagine what they were worth today. Tilley had finally regained consciousness and grinned as she advised the two of them that her "financial advisor" would be happy to assist them in any way he could when they decided what they wanted to do with them. He also suggested they get the cards appraised and insured as quickly as possible.

Once the jubilation had subsided, they found themselves completely emotionally spent and didn't even have the strength to lift their glasses to make one more toast. Dalton did that "man-hug" thing with Gene and expressed how delighted he was that he was there to share this with them and said that he couldn't wait to tell his dad. Jordan approached Gene almost cautiously, but with a big hug she conveyed the fact that she felt the same way.

After a few seconds Gene carefully backed away from Jordan's embrace, but while still holding her hands he confessed, "I'm sure glad you found out how I feel about you before I knew you were rich . . . I wouldn't want you to think I was just after your money."

That lightened the mood in the room as the four of them proceeded to share in a little "happy dance" before collapsing in exhaustion.

As they all relaxed and reveled in the good news, Tilley sighed and asked Jordan if she still believed that destiny had nothing to do with it.

Ah yes, there was that ever-present look of skepticism that Tilley had grown to know and love, then Jordan came back with her rebuttal.

"Are you telling me that some greater force made my dad want to make an informed and educated decision to invest in his children's' future?"

"Not at all." Tilley admitted. "But what about the *big* picture? It's all about the choices *we* made."

"What do you mean?" Dalton asked.

"Well, take a look at what brought us all here together to this very moment. What choices had to be made to ensure that these events would take place?"

Now they *all* looked puzzled and waited as they *knew* she was going to explain.

Tilley sat up and cleared her throat so she could enlighten them. "Look at what *had* to happen before this journey could even begin? If you hadn't been touched by that little boy and his sister crossing the street that day, you wouldn't have made the *choice* to start the search for Dalton. If you hadn't, then you wouldn't have made the *choice* to call me. If I hadn't *chosen* to be here to "break the ice" so to speak between you and Gene, he might never had been aware of your search and therefore he wouldn't have made the *choice* to tell Dalton about your situation . . . not to mention the fact that you two would still be playing that little "cat and mouse" game for who knows *how* much longer. You *chose* to return to your home town where we found the boxes that held the documents that have now changed your life. If you hadn't, who knows *when* that envelope in the scrapbook would have been discovered? Dalton, the day we meet at your office you said you weren't even supposed to be in town. What if you had *chosen* to go to that seminar and someone else from your office assisted us? You may never have seen that picture we had of your family and who knows what would have happened then?"

They couldn't argue with her logic because it was all true. One thing led to another which led up to them all being there at that moment.

As the three of them looked at each other as if waiting for the other one to find the words to refute her explanation, Tilley sat up, and while poring herself *another* glass of wine was the first one to break the hush that had come over the room, "What was it that kept you from going out of town that day anyway?"

Dalton seemed very relaxed as he answered her question and while munching on a cheese a cracker snack he took from the tray of goodies in front of him he explained. "My entire staff knows that if anything comes up concerning my home town that I want to handle it personally. We had an application for funds to help repair the roof at St. Augustus Church. Apparently they received an anonymous donation that was more than enough to cover the cost of the repairs. They were able to start construction immediately so they rescinded that request and made a new application for a grant to start a daycare instead. In order to receive the funding, they would have to have qualified staff so our foundation will send someone to train whoever they choose in order to be properly certified, then we can help expedite the grant application on their behalf."

"So you *chose* to forego the seminar and handle their application yourself." Tilley said matter-of-factly.

"I see where you're going with this now." He commented as he nodded his head with a grin and a look of understanding.

"Wait a minute!" Jordan said rather loudly and spun around to face her aunt. "St. Augustus Church? You said you had to use a land-line!"

Tilley sheepishly put her head down to avert Jordan's accusing stare, then sat up to defend herself. "It was the truth! I had to get my financial advisor on the phone so he could get the proper information from the Vicar in order to transfer the funds - not something I wanted to do on a cell phone."

Dalton sprang upright and pointed a finger at Tilley, "*You* made the anonymous donation?!"

"Oh sweetie, it was *such* a great apple pie." Tilley said as she closed her eyes and slowly sniffed the air as if she was back in Grace's kitchen. Then she came back to earth with, "I just wanted to repay Grace and Ira for their hospitality." As she sat back looking rather pleased with herself she said, "I rest my case."

Then she pointed out, "Because of the *choices* each of us made, we were all destined to be here together to share the legacy that your parents left you. Without that little boy, you wouldn't have me here. Without me – you wouldn't have Gene . . . or the *now* not-so-anonymous donation that keep Dalton in town. Without Gene – you wouldn't have Dalton or Sarah. Without Sarah, you wouldn't have known about your mother. Without Grace and Ira, you wouldn't have, well let's just say that thanks to them, you are now . . . "stinking rich"!"

EPILOGUE

A lot has happened since that day they discovered the contents of the mystery boxes. Jordan and Gene got engaged so Tilley introduced Sarah to Eric, the guy who lives down the hall. Melinda returned with the news that she had been disinherited but after learning of Dalton's good fortune her family is now begging her forgiveness and the two of them have decided to let them squirm for a while. Dalton paid to have the best doctors in the world consult on Gene's brother's condition while Tilley brought in a faith healer from the Philippines. Regardless of whose medicine worked, he's now making a remarkable recovery. Due to the fact that neither one of them spend as much time as they used to at their businesses; Dalton promoted Jody to Director of the foundation, Gene promoted Sarah to manager of the bistro, and both are flourishing. Tilley has given up her globe-trotting in order spend time with her family and write her memories, so now they take "family" vacations *together*. Jordan doesn't argue with Tilley any more when she talks about karma, fate, or accepting signs of destiny, after all, it's still about the choices *we* make that determine the outcome, and sometimes . . . miracles do happen.

Even though they *thought* they had it all figured out, in actuality they had overlooked one very important variable in the equation. It was the decision that young man on the bicycle made when he *chose* to ride his bike to a job interview that day instead of taking the bus. He didn't leave himself enough time which made him late, which caused him to be careless, which put him in front of Jordan's bumper at the stop sign. The *choice* he made that day may have virtually had no effect on him, short of a couple of bruised shins, but the cascading effect of the events that were created as a result of his decision changed Jordan and her family's lives forever.

So whose hands does our destiny *really* lie in?

8504232R0

Made in the USA
Charleston, SC
15 June 2011